W9-ADB-237

NEW JACK RABBIT CITY

STARRING THE

Chicago Hares

NEW JACK RABBIT CITY

IT'S THE FREQUENCY

THE FREQUENCY

TUNE IN

I wish I could say we were headed "down the rabbit hole,"

but this was a whole lot more.

NEW JACK RABBIT CITY

Starring

The Chicago Hares

by

Michael Evanouski

and

Gail Galvan

Story by Michael Evanouski and Gail Galvan
Graphics by Michael Evanouski
Lyrics by Gail Galvan and Michael Evanouski
Music by DanoSongs.com (Dan O'Connor)
Voice by Gail Galvan

Visit www.newjackrabbitcity.podomatic.com to listen to original songs:

>
> One Sunny Day
> Rappin' Rabbits (A Change of Hearts)
> Rush Crush
> King Caponey
> Putz (I'm Livin' the Good Life Now)
> The Chase
> Love Sparks (Wrigley, I Love You)
> Love Conquers All
> Bronzey and Meigs (Dreams Got a Way of Findin' You)
> A Million Songs (Lyrics only)

Contacts for information:
ggpodbooks@hotmail.com   mike@goliveidaho.com

Dedication

Dedicated to the preservation of the creative spirit. Also, to partners in storytelling who believe in their sparks of literary imagination, then proceed to: foster, nurture, and persevere for the sake of imagination and entertainment.

Acknowledgments

Gratitude abounds in our hearts for the universal positive forces of the world, namely God and other spiritual connections, along with the wondrous powers of: intuition, creativity, and love.

Special thanks to our families and friends for their love and support.

The authors wish to thank each other for being there, believing, and offering never-ending encouragement.

We'd also like to thank: hares, rabbits, Chicago, Idaho, Abby, Zach, and the dogs, Eggy (Eggnacio/Tonto) and Nache (Nasty), for the inspiration.

Thanks also to a talented writer friend, Jane Burns, for her keen advice and assistance with regard to story development. Work continued after her help and input into this literary project. So any errors or imperfections—that "credit" goes to the authors.

Eternal thanks to the miracle age of Internet resources, electronic publishing, and publishers, especially CreateSpace, for this book! "Oh, what a wonderful world!"

We must also give credit to Sharon Palmeri, founder of Write-On Hoosiers, for first publishing chapter one of N.J.R.C. in the 2012 edition of *Hoosier Horizon Magazine*. Thanks Sharon!

To DanoSongs.com (Dan O'Connor) for his precious gift, the music. Our story sings because of you and your tunes. We are forever grateful!

Alas, to Ebooklaunch.com for being there—thanks for helping us with the blastoff of our Ebook on Kindle.

CONTENTS

Dedication

Acknowledgments

Prologue

Chapter

Epilogue

"It was magical, this moment: the last step before turning back, the dawn that's always rising, the sun that never sets. A spin of reality, the glimpse of what can be—a tunnel into the open mind."

–Uncle Mike

"Spend the day with the sun,
the night with the moon,
your dreams awaiting to come true.
If you never wish, if you never dream,
you'll never truly let yourself be you."

–Rush Palmer

Prologue

I surprised myself when I said I'd follow Abby, my niece, to some alleged magical kingdom to meet a tall, talking rabbit. Talking rabbits living among humans? To me, it sounded like the old classic fictional rabbit story, *Harvey,* with Jimmy Stewart. But this was no Pooka from old Celtic mythology, nor Lewis Carroll's white rabbit.

How was I going to handle this? Pretend I see her imaginary friend, or what? I've always loved her enthusiasm and wild imagination, but I know there is a fine line sometimes that adults have to draw for kids between reality and make-believe. But it was only a one mile hike for Abby, Zach, the dogs and me. One afternoon, as the hot sand slowly cooled and the wind settled quietly with the sunshine and a few clouds above us, we headed out for a place called New Jack Rabbit City.

I'm Mike, by the way. Born a Hoosier, in Indiana, I moved to Idaho years ago and just love it. I live in a world of wonderment, surrounded by natural beauty that changes by the moment. Lucky me, I'm married to my fun-loving, adventurous wife, Lori. Hike, bike, ski, kayak, climb mountains—you name it, we do it. Idaho is an awesome place to explore.

Our house is filled with love and laughter, especially with our beloved pets always adding to the excitement. I really enjoy my extended family, too, and spend a lot of time with an energetic, bright nephew and niece.

Zach is twelve, loves the dogs, teases, but puts up with his younger sister. He sort of lives in his own world, but just lately we did go fishing a couple of times. He's funny, a fast learner, and boy can he skip rocks.

Abby's only eight, but she's a bit more assertive. In fact, she's the one who led us on our hike that one sunny day to the lake behind the observatory. Blonde, sweet, giggly and always using big words or teaching me something, Abby is a constant storyteller of folklore and tall tales. I like to compare her to Dr. Van Helsing, the fictional character from the Bram Stoker novel, *Tracking Down Vampires,* since she's quite the keen tracker, too. Only her specialty is giant rabbits.

For some reason, as we hiked along that day, a Van Morrison song kept playing in my head. I mouthed the lyrics:

> *"We were born before the wind*
> *Also younger than the sun...*
> *Let your soul and spirit fly into the mystic..."*

Little did I know, in the next few days, how those words would ring so true and change our lives forever. You know how when something really bad happens to someone and that person always says, "I never thought it would happen to me, but it did?" Well, when unexplained, miraculous or magical occurrences happen to people, like it did to us, we couldn't believe it happened either. But it did. I wish I could say we were headed "down the rabbit hole," but this was a whole lot more.

We Begin

Shimmering in its own reflection, the big sand dune outside Bruneau, Idaho, towers four hundred and seventy feet above the lake. As we hiked along, our feet made imprints on the moist sand with each step we took on the beach circling a smaller lake. We hung around for thirty minutes at that rabbit beachhead. Zach pitched sticks as the dogs slammed the water and fetched.

Before arriving at the beach, we'd passed large fields of cabbage grass growing right in the springs that flowed into the lake. Bright green and soaked in spring water; it served as summer feed for the jacks. The hike continued along a narrow lane between thickets and saw grass.

Finally, we came to a wooden post sticking out of the sand and the sign on it read: *Jack Rabbits Only.* Abby looked to the left, then to the right, and said, "Hey, we don't play by the rules." Then, in a hushed voice, "Jackrabbits with those telescoping ears can use them as antennae. Whisper only." We hiked on.

Abby informed us again, "Like I've told you before, the giant rabbit Mayor here is six-feet-tall."

Zach and I rolled our eyes – we couldn't help it. Then I thought to myself, this I gotta see. Followers we were that day; so off we trekked forward down a path, just right of the beach, right down the middle of New Jack Rabbit City.

As we left the beach, the wet dogs shook themselves off on my pants, and sprayed the willows that boxed us in on two sides. We carried our shoes, after shaking out all the sand. I remember making the comment, "One thing you got to say about these jacks, they must love this sand." Then Abby told us we were close. She could tell because of the "empty beach and tracks" we were following, supposedly.

It was like being in a tunnel. A stream graced us on one side and the lake on the other. In the stream, the cabbage grass grew as green as emeralds and flowed silently in the current; its leaves floated in a watery space. Willows arched above us, as we suspiciously moved along.

I had to ask, "*New* Jack Rabbit City? What's up with the old city?"

This brings me to the story of the original Jack Rabbit City, which Abby related that pastoral spring evening. Located in the sands and sagebrush behind the dunes, which we skirted that day, was the spot where the jacks used to live.

Here's what she told us. "A hundred years ago, the jacks had it easy: water, food, and no one would wander off the beaten path to this piece of nowhere. Until the water dried up! It was in the early Fifties." She stared off and spoke as if she'd traveled back in time and could see it all right then and there.

"It was the irrigators. They dried up the pond, so the water was all gone, and there was no more sweet grass like we see rippling in the stream now."

Earlier in the day, we'd passed large green fields of sugar beets, alfalfa, clover, and mint. Apparently, what was good for the farmers turned out bad for the jacks. It was move or die, so the jacks moved their city.

No sooner had Abby finished her story, and a flurry stirred up, riding on a breeze blowing down the dune—white blossoms, or seeds, or something filled the air almost like snow. I thought to myself, "What this place must be like in winter!" Zach and I jerked our heads toward Abby in disbelief, or a newfound belief. Then the path opened and a second sign read: *Welcome to New Jack Rabbit City.*

What a difference a day makes! What a difference that day made in our lives. In the magical days ahead, we would learn all about altered realities. After all, "seeing is believing." Abby had accomplished her mission—led us right to Mr. Mayor, the giant puzzle piece within the mystical kingdom mystery.

From his talking lips to our unbelieving ears, we learned all about the artesian well water, how it enabled hares and rabbits to grow big and tall. And that's not all! When the digital frequency changes came about, another miraculous transformation occurred. Before rabbits and hares even knew what was happening, their extra frontal lobe brain waves kept developing.

It wasn't long before: speaking, reasoning, and an incredible metamorphosis had changed their lives forever. Walking became a choice. Often they hopped, but standing upright became as easy as breathing. They even learned to adapt, use their wrists and paws in various ways so they could clutch bottles and pick up things more easily. Though not as agile and capable as raccoons when it came to opening or carrying things, life was becoming easier and easier every day.

Some Chicago hares tuned in, too, packed up and moved west to New Jack Rabbit City. It's a wonderland tale, one for the storybooks. Let us, the human family lucky enough to witness it all, share it with you. Like anyone who is bold enough to chase a dream, as many of the characters in this story do—feel free to live the adventure. But don't be fooled at first. No new paradise existence comes easy. Social and personal betterment is always challenged and often sabotaged by the counterattacking adversarial forces of the world, any world—even a magical kingdom.

ONE SUNNY DAY

I believe in magic now, I believe, I believe.
Can't tell me it doesn't happen, just believe,
just believe.
I believe in magic now, I believe, I believe.
Can't tell me it doesn't happen, just believe,
just believe.

The Bruneau sky lights up my life.
I run in the sand with Zach and Uncle Mike.
Bruneau, Bruneau, one sunny day,
life's never been the same—
no way, no way.
Not since Mr. Mayor showed up
that one sunny day, that one sunny day.

I believe in magic now, I believe, I believe.
Can't tell me it doesn't happen, just believe,
just believe.
I believe in magic now, I believe, I believe.
Can't tell me it doesn't happen, just believe,
just believe.

We wandered into a magical place.
The six-feet-tall rabbit had a grin on his face.
Everything changed on that one sunny day.
Life's never been the same—
no way, no way, not since that one sunny day.

Mr. Mayor spoke perfect English.
He even tipped his hat.
We said, "What's that? What's that?
What's that?"
We couldn't believe our eyes.
Thought our minds were playing tricks on us
until we said our goodbyes.

But there he stood with his flashy clothes
and funny shoes,
petting our dogs and giving us clues
about how he grew so extra tall.
And that's not all, that's not all.
He told us how he tuned in one day.
Ever since then, he's sure had a lot to say.

Life's never been the same—
no way, no way.
Everything changed on that one sunny day.
With New Jack Rabbit City, that magical place,
Mr. Mayor, with the grin on his face.
One sunny day, one sunny day,
life's never been the same—
no way, no way, not since that one sunny day.

I believe in magic now, I believe, I believe.
Can't tell me it doesn't happen, just believe, just believe.
I believe in magic now, I believe, I believe.
Can't tell me it doesn't happen, just believe, just believe.

Wow! Talking rabbits. Wow!
Can you hear them? Wow!

Maybe you can you hear them?
Wow. Talking rabbits.
I believe in magic now, I believe, I believe.
Can't tell me it doesn't happen, just believe, just believe.

Chapter One: Buckinghams on the Move

"Your dad told you to pack up your stuff," Miranda said, "and that's the last time we're going to tell you, Son. We're movin' out west to Idaho and that's it. And don't forget that other sack of carrots in the garage, the ones our neighbor, Sallywig, brought us." After her stern orders, Miranda hopped closer to Bobbiteer Buckingham and stroked her son's grey, furry ears with a mother's affectionate touch. She felt proud that he was the spitting image of his parents, only a smaller version: healthy, good-looking, and strong, especially his hind leg muscles. If only he had the happiness in his heart, she thought to herself.

"But Mom," Bobbiteer pouted, pulling away.

"Son, you'll live. You know your father when he makes up his mind. He says there's a better life for us there, a new Mayor, a sand dune town, and even kids and dogs that get along with hares like us. Now go!"

Bobbiteer hopped away a few yards; then turned back ready to argue that he didn't want to leave his friends behind: Tazzy and, especially, Beatledoo. They'd never get to watch the Bears play ever again, he lamented to himself. Mom and Dad couldn't know what this would do to a young hare, up and moving away. Besides, Idaho? Shoot, they just handed over one of their best college football players to Chicago. Bobbiteer was sure the star footballer didn't want to move to Chicago any more than he wanted to go to Idaho. Poor Bobbiteer just kept mumbling, pouting and staggering around like a little lost lamb. Another terrible thought: No more Wrigley's Field or baseball seasons here. He kept hopping away toward the garage, until he heard his father's voice. "Miranda, are you ready to go?" Wyndhameer stroked the fur on her back; then asked in a more commanding voice, "Where is he? Is he still grumbling? Sometimes, I swear, I liked it better before the frequency kicked in, when our son couldn't talk and carry on." Bobbiteer mustered up enough courage to hop back quickly, position himself directly in front of his father, and plead his case.

"Dad, I think you're making a big mistake. This town, it could be just a ghost town for all we know. I'd rather stay here with my friends. You can drop me off at Aunt Janetto's. Please, please Dad!" He bent both his ears forward – and wiggled his nose – then took a deep breath, hoping for a miraculous affirmative answer.

"I'm sorry, Son. You'll see. It's for the best. I know change is difficult, Bobbit, but adaptation is what life is all about. I'm sorry you have to leave your friends. I know that's the most difficult thing about this. But I promise you that new friends and exciting adventures await us in New Jack Rabbit City. Now grab your backpack and carrots and let's go. We've gotta hop on that freight train before it heads out."

"But Dad," Bobbiteer whined.

"Son, think about it. So many of our friends in cages, rats in the alleyways, rabbit poachers, gangs running around this city at night trying to catch and sell us like slaves again. Maybe humans can enjoy the luxuries of Chicago, but it's no place for hares like us. The city's no place to raise a rabbit or hare. I've made up my mind."

Bobbiteer knew his life was over. He just knew it. He'd never be happy ever, ever again.

After Wyndhameer gave his final speech and directives to hit the road, he patted Bobbiteer on the head, picked up the loaded backpacks filled with the Buckingham's family belongings, and led the way toward the tracks. Bobbiteer got one last glimpse of Wrigley Field. Soon, dusk in Chicago set in and all the bright lights made the big city look pretty again. But the wise hare knew better.

He whispered, almost loud enough for Miranda and Bobbiteer to hear. "Too much sham and drudgery. No, we're out of here, headed for the quiet, beautiful welcoming sand dunes of Idaho."

Chapter Two:
Raccoon Rogues and Nightmare Chills

As the freight train traveled westward on the railroad tracks, Riley the raccoon gave the order to his mischievous buddy: "When I conk old rabbit-ears there on the head, you grab the backpack, okay?"

"Okay, yeah I got this. I can't believe they didn't know we were here, hiding. It's been a while since we cleaned up," Rowlie confessed, as he sniffed his mostly black, smelly fur.

"All right, here we go." Riley crept forward from behind a bunch of boxes and snuck up behind Wyndhameer, who sat resting up against an old barrel. Just as he lunged at Wyndhameer, swinging a big stick, something jabbed his right shin and he slammed down on the floor.

Rowlie got scared and ran back for cover.

"Dad, look, I got him!" Bobbiteer said proudly. His mother jumped up quickly and tried to hug her son, but he stood firm in his fighting stance, ready to attack the raccoon again if necessary.

Wyndhameer turned with a grin, "Good job, Son, that wink of an eye did pretty good for us, didn't it? Nothing like a wink for communicating something important. And you, behind the boxes, get your butt out here, too!"

Rowlie sheepishly walked forward, his head hanging down.

Riley Raccoon stood up and looked at the young hare and said, "What are you, some kind of karate-kicking kid or something? Hey, we wasn't gonna hurt ya. We're just hungry. We was smellin' those carrots. You think you could spare a few?"

"You were gonna steal our backpack! Thieves! My dad would never let you get away with that! Right Dad? Me neither!"

"Okay, Son, apparently what we have here are a couple of hungry raccoons. I suppose if we hand over a few carrots, you'll be on your merry way, is that right?"

"Oh yes, Big Rabbit," Riley replied. "We'd be much obliged. Right out of your hair – and I ain't trying to pun ya. Train's slowin' down, we can get off right here."

"What do you think, dear? Do you think these thugs deserve a couple of carrots?" Wyndhameer wiggled his nose and cocked an ear.

"Wyn, I'm glad you and Bobs are okay. These rascals better promise not to go trying to hurt anyone else. If they promise, then yes, a few carrots might be in order." Miranda reached for the backpack with the carrots.

"Oh yes, ma'am, we promise," the two raccoons chimed in while holding out their grubby paws. "It was just the hunger pains, ma'am," Rowlie added, as honestly as he could.

"Okay then, here you go. Off with you now." That was the last of the pesky raccoons. They hopped off the train and scampered toward their next scheming adventure, whatever that would be.

"Mom, why do raccoons have such black color around their eyes?" Bobbiteer asked.

"Well, Son, I think it's probably a way for them to be less noticeable at night while they are doing their roaming around. Not sure though."

"Hmm. I don't like raccoons. They're sneaky."

"Oh, Bobbit, they were just trying to survive, but there are more honorable ways."

That was just the start of a brand new day for the Buckingham hares. Bobbiteer liked the adventure, he felt like a Ninja Turtle warrior. He hoped more thieves would come along so he could really lay some karate chops on them. By sundown, the three Buckinghams were exhausted and stiff from riding on the train all night and day. Bobbiteer liked hearing the train whistle blow at times, but he hated the other clamoring noises and jostling around.

"Are we there yet, Mom?"

"No, Son, we've got a ways to go yet, and we'll be stopping off in Denver to see some relatives, so they can find us a connection. The Rocky Mountains, you'll like those, so get some rest while you can, honey." She patted him on his forehead. Bobbiteer hated it when she did that. Not the patting, calling him "honey."

While his mom and dad took turns keeping watch, Bobbiteer slept like a baby bunny. However, he didn't dream like one. Since his dad was always hinting that things were a lot tougher for rabbits and hares at one time, he could only imagine what he was talking about. His dreams did a good job of showing him the dark side of humanity.

There he was, back home on Rush Street, in the alleyway behind his dad's favorite Italian restaurant, the one he always talked about. He'd said there'd been some good times, even during the worst of it. Good old Adolph's.

But it sure wasn't 2012. More like the Fifties or Sixties. Oh man, he thought, it's cold and dark. Must be ten below zero. He wondered why he was all alone, Rush Street was always busy. "Chicago lives at night, more so than by day." That's what his dad always said. Bobbiteer's teeth chattered, and he felt icicles on his toes. In fact, they were turning dark blue. He shivered like never before and wished with all his heart that his mom was right there in front of him, patting him on the head and calling him "honey."

"What's that?" A loud noise startled him.

Frightened to death, he looked over at Adolph's as the back door opened. Out stepped baseball heroes Ernie Banks and Ron Santo, right in front of him. He couldn't believe it, but his dad had said you could meet all kinds of famous people hanging out at Adolph's. He remembered one story about the time when Frank Sinatra almost stepped on his dad, how Sinatra turned out to be nice and reached down and gave him a few kind strokes and said he was sorry. Oh, and the Smothers Brothers, and Phyllis Diller! That stuck in Bobbiteer's head. His father always said to never forget the best medicine in the world: laughter. Well, second to love, that is.

Bobbiteer could hear his dad's words clearly, "Son, life's going to be a mixture of great joy, and sadly, much sorrow. But laughter and love, those are your life jackets. Don't ever forget that. Okay, Son? Believe me, it will help someday. And whatever you do, don't ever give up your freedom. We hares and rabbits have fought too long and hard for any of us to succumb to slavery and cages. Never again."

"Hey you! You there!"

Bobbiteer blinked and in an instant Ernie Banks and Ron Santo had disappeared, and been replaced by a giant policeman in a blue uniform, with a gun pointed at him. The young hare closed his eyes real hard and ground his teeth. After a few seconds he opened them again and there stood a five-foot raccoon in front of him, carrying Bobbiteer's backpack.

"Hey, you're that Riley Raccoon. Gimme that back! It's mine!"

He grabbed at it, but as he did the raccoon shrunk to the size of a mouse and the backpack fell to the ground, becoming a pile of ashes. Bobbiteer walked down the alleyway. Haunting, howling animal screams were coming from a warehouse building down the street. He knew he should stay away, but he just had to see what was going on. He found a squeaky, grey steel door open just enough for him to squeeze through.

The horror of the sight overwhelmed him. Hundreds of cages, filled with trapped, sick dying rabbits. He threw up three times due to the smell and injustice. This must be what his dad was talking about, how they used to have to live in cages and be treated like slaves just so more and more bunnies could be... manual? Manufated. No, "manufactured," that was the word he used. Manufactured! Yeah, so bunnies could be manufactured and sold to some kid around Easter, to be used as a toy. And half the time, three weeks later, the bunnies were back in cages like this. He threw up again, and his throat got so dry he couldn't breathe.

He ran out the door and he kept running, and then he was at the Navy Pier, which was locked in ice. He couldn't stand it anymore and just knew it must be a nightmare.

"Please, God, let me wake up," he begged.

No luck. Bobbiteer closed his eyes again, tightly. When he opened them, the Pier and storefront images before him began to disappear. The frozen water was next.

"Bobbit! Bobbit! Honey, dear, wake up. WAKE UP!" Miranda shook her son again, trying to snap him out of whatever awful nightmare he was in. "Son, look, you've got to see these beautiful mountains. Look!" It worked. Bobbiteer's eyes flashed open.

"Mom! Oh God, I'm back! Oh Mom, it was awful." He tried to hold back the tears but just couldn't.

Miranda hugged her son and said, "Another one, hmm? It's okay, Bobs. It was a nightmare, only a bad dream. I'm right here."

"Mom, I was so scared. I never want to live in a cage. Promise me I'll never have to live in a cage." He hugged her.

"I promise you, Bobs; that will never happen. Now c'mon, take a look, this is Colorado. It's beautiful country and there are some great big mountains right over there – look!"

"WOW! Those are cool! Do hares live in the mountains?"

"Sometimes. Many live on ranches. Some in the city, and yeah, others live in the foothills and mountains. We're just about to Uncle Blake's place. See if he can find us a connection to Idaho. So try to wake up now, okay?"

"We're here, hon, this is where we get off," Wyndhameer said. He gathered up the backpacks, but Miranda insisted on carrying one.

Bobbiteer jumped up and down and with a big smile on his face shouted enthusiastically, "Colorado, boy am I glad to see you!"

Chapter Three: Runaways Rush and Ryker Palmer

Although running away is always a dangerous idea for a teenager, that's exactly what Rush Palmer planned to do. Back in Chicago, the Buckinghams weren't the only rabbits heading west.

"I know what you're gonna do, Sis. You're not the only one who sneaks on Jeffrey's computer at the house. I know how to push down on a fake mouse, put a pen in my mouth and type like humans, too. I saw just what his friend, Zach, from Idaho, sent him. I saw the message. You believe in that stuff? A whole new town of rabbits – and six-feet-tall ones, really? And I thought *I* was the dreamer."

He warned his big sister, "Mom will go crazy when she knows you're gone, and when she finds you—you'll be in soooo much trouble!"

"Shut up and get out of my room!" Rush shooed him like a fly toward the door.

"Sis, I know I'm a lot younger than you, but you better listen to me. This is stupid. Just stupid," Ryker persisted.

Rush kept shoving clothes into her backpack. Then she picked up her music box, a small carousel her dad bought her for her last birthday, and tucked it away, too. She never even took off her birthstone necklace, not once, since he had clasped it around her neck before his final kiss goodbye one day back in time, the day Raffaello Palmer died of a sudden heart attack.

"Listen, you little sneak. I love you, little brother, but I'm leaving and there is nothing you or Mom can do about it. You'll see. Mom's killing herself here working two jobs and for what? Just so we can keep up with the McCormicks? I don't want to live like this, not anymore. I want to spend time with her, go to the beach, the movies, just sit outside and talk, like we used to. All she talks about now is how she's got to keep the money coming in so we can stay put here on the Gold Coast, and go to some fancy college. I mean, I like it here sometimes, but not if it's going to kill Mom."

She looked in a nearby mirror, wiped away a few tears with her right paw and tried to put a smile on her light brown and tan-colored face while she scratched her pure white stomach. "Besides, our grandparents were of European descent. We don't belong in the city.

We need to get back to a more peaceful, natural habitat. And that's all I'm gonna say about it!"

"Yeah but…" Ryker trailed off as he bounced on Rush's fancy bed, the centerpiece of her stylish bedroom.

A human family of four had fixed it all up for the Palmers one summer, so the hare family would stay. Jeffrey, the ten year old human computer geek, loved rabbits and hares, and treated them well. He was always receiving interesting messages, popular songs, and new video game information from his friend, Zach, out in Idaho, and sharing them with Rush. Lately, though, he didn't know if Zach needed reality medication or if a magic city really did exist. He kept asking for a picture for proof, but hadn't received it. Zach swore that he had finally captured a couple photos of the character they called Mr. Mayor, the giant-sized rabbit who supposedly wore clothes and talked. But every time the film got developed, nothing. Just pure black.

"No, this is it," Rush persisted, "I'm going to New Jack Rabbit City and that's final! Mom will come after me, with you, I suppose. Then she'll see how much nicer it is out west. She'll find love again, and an easier job, I just know it! They say the sun shines three hundred days out of the year there. But don't you dare try to follow me on your own."

Ryker whined, but to no avail. Rush had her mind made up.

It was her girlfriend, Sheddy, who came up with the idea that Rush could ride out with someone her host family knew. Mr. Kauffey was in the trucking business, and he was leaving today, going west. He owned a flatbed, and Sheddy found out he was hauling a big doghouse all the way to Denver for some friend who had just gotten a new dog. After all, it wasn't doing Sheddy's host family any good, since they had to give up Freddy, their beloved Yorkshire Terrier. (At least they found him a good home.) Sheddy swore if she could burn down places and buildings that did not allow dogs, without getting caught or hurting anyone, she would.

"You're crazy, Sis. Hitchin' a ride in a doghouse on the back of a flatbed? I mean really?"

"Take care of mom. You can tell her, *after* I've gone, about our new home in New Jack Rabbit City. That's in Idaho, you got it? Under my mattress, that's where the rest of the information is, you're good at telling on me, so show her that, but only after I'm gone, okay?" Rush couldn't resist a small sign of affection for her brother, so she stroked his left ear; then hoisted the backpack over her right shoulder and headed out the door.

Ryker pouted and plunked back down on the bed. He reached down and pulled out the paper his sister had left, found some other scratch paper, then scribbled a little note telling his mom not to worry, he'd take care of Rush, and left their destination information on the bed. He hopped quickly to his room, grabbed a few belongings, including a small-framed picture he had of his once intact family, father and all; then did exactly what his sister told him not to. He followed her.

After all, Dad left him in charge when he'd said, "If anything ever happens to me, you're the man of the house. Okay pal? We named you Ryker for a reason, Son. It means Knight. So you take care of your mom and sister. It's just the facts, I've got this heart condition and I'm not going to live forever, so I'm counting on you." That meant Ryker had to protect his sister, so he tailed her into the city.

Sheddy lived near a John Hancock high-rise condo, and it didn't take long for Rush to hop over there, from street to historic street, ducking behind buildings and into alleyways whenever she thought it necessary. Ryker followed behind and stayed out of sight. He was good. "Quiet as an Indian," Dad used to say. His dad taught him everything he needed to know to avoid the gangs – the North-Siders and the South-Siders – and the other bad elements of the big, windy city. "Play it safe, Son, safety first, then you can forget the negatives and enjoy the positives a big city has to offer." Ryker didn't really know all the negatives out there, but he knew he had to avoid cars like the rabbit plague.

Before Rush left town, she needed to talk to Wrigley, her bad boy reputation hare boyfriend, who she had fallen in love with two months ago. She had to go into the city, anyway, to pick up something important for her mom, a locket. Wrigley had made a copy of a photo for Rush. Now she and her mom would have identical ones.

When she showed up though, the South-Sider gang, who Wrigley just happened to be a member of, gave her a real hard time, especially the gang's boss Caponey, who gave up on believing in romantic love so long ago. He cracked jokes and harassed both Wrigley and Rush while they tried to have a private conversation – you know, the kind when two lovers vow their love forever and ever.

Caponey grabbed the locket from Rush as she'd clasped it in her right hand, and threw it sky high. Luckily, Wrigley caught it just in time. Then Caponey and the rest of the gang members teased and teased the two and even pulled at Rush's fur. Wrigley almost slugged Caponey for that wrong move.

Ryker hid behind a garbage dumpster and tried to remain calm. He knew he couldn't take them all, but he was ready to jump out and do something, anything, to try and help his sister. Thankfully, it looked like her boyfriend would take care of her, so Ryker stayed put until things calmed down. Then, while Rush was saying her final tearful goodbye, he headed over to Sheddy's so he could get there before her.

Rush couldn't understand why Wrigley wouldn't pack up and leave with her, right then and there, especially after he had handed her a photo of the two of them taken a few days ago. They looked so happy and were perfect together, she thought. He was about the same color, but taller, and strong. She liked that.

Wrigley got real evasive, though, and just kept saying he'd be right behind her, but he had to stay and take care of something important first.

"Fine," Rush said, with tears in her eyes. "Just stay here then. I don't care if you ever come out. Mom was right, all you care about is that stupid gang of yours. I care for you, Wrigley, but until you change, that's *if* you can ever change, I just give up. I don't want to see you. It's me or your stupid hoodlums. I see some good in them but when they all gang together, they're just awful. If they mean more to you than I do...."

"But Rush, you don't understand. I've got to stay here, just a little longer. I promise it's for a good reason. I will be out there in no time. I'll get a chance to talk to your mother. I love you Rush Palmer. You are my wild rose and the reason I feel hope and joy. I'm always going to love you, forever. Please believe me. There's just something I have to do first." Wrigley tried to kiss her but she pulled away quickly.

"I gotta go. Sheddy said my ride is leaving pretty soon. I don't want to miss it. Goodbye Wrigley." She turned and hopped away.

When Rush arrived, her friend Sheddy shouted, "C'mon, Rush, hurry! Jump in the back in the doghouse so he doesn't see you. He's getting ready to leave! He's only going to Denver for some business before dropping off the doghouse, that's as far as he can get you. I'm sorry, Rush, I thought my mom said he was going to see his Uncle

Sherlock in Idaho. But I guess his plans changed. You are cutting it awfully close!"

"That's okay, I'll go to my aunt's house; she's in Denver. Hey, can you call my mom and tell her NOT to call the Rabbit Patrol, just come out to Idaho, too, okay? I'll be waiting for her. Please tell her that, all right? Oh, and tell her I picked up the locket, okay?"

"Yeah, yeah. Sure. Now hurry up!" Sheddy quickly, but gently, pushed Rush toward the back of the flatbed. "He's coming. Hurry, Mr. Kauffey is coming out! Bye, write to me. Be careful and good luck!" She hopped away to hide behind a bush. She had heard that Mr. Kauffey wasn't very fond of rabbits. Rush flung her backpack onto the flatbed, then jumped up, grabbed it, and peeked into the doghouse.

"BOO!" shouted Ryker as he stuck his head out. He was prepared for anything his sister would say to talk him out of going.

"Oh for rabbit's sakes alive!" Rush yelled as she jumped back, falling on her butt.

"Sorry, Sis, Dad said I was the boss now, so here I am, to serve and protect." Ryker stared at her, feeling extremely proud of himself.

"Dad never said, 'Boss.' Now, get down. I don't have time to argue with you. Here comes Mr. Kauffey. Get in the doghouse and zip it shut, you little brat." Rush climbed in after him, and within minutes they were off on their adventure, traveling west on the expressway with cars and trucks whizzing by like killer tornado winds. The noise was so loud, Rush placed her paws over her ears.

"Is this the Dan Ryan, Sis?"

"I don't know, shut up – it's one expressway or another, but you shouldn't be here! I can't believe this. Don't you ever listen to what me or Mom tells you?"

"No. I do what my tuned in smart brain tells me to do!"

"It was a rhetorical question, brainless brother, no need to answer. I know you always do whatever you want." Rush squirmed, trying to get comfortable. She thought she'd have the doghouse all to herself.

"Well, you're a girl. You need protection," Ryker said, absolutely sure of his job and capabilities.

"Just what I need, a little squirt thinking he's my bodyguard."

"You got it, that's me, just like in that movie."

"What movie?"

"*The Bodyguard.* Nobody's gonna hurt my sister," Ryker said defiantly.

"Fine, I give up. Just stay low, okay? Stay out of trouble!"

"No problem. Now where are we going again? Idaho?"

"Nope. Denver, I guess. Sheddy said Mr. Kauffey's plans changed. He isn't going all the way to Idaho, so we'll have to figure out what to do when we get to Denver. I swear, Ryker, you better keep out of sight or you're going to mess everything up," she ordered. Then she begged. "Pleeease?"

"Sure, Rush, it'll be okay. Don't worry so much. We'll make it, check out the new town, then figure out some way to get Mom out there. *If* she doesn't catch the very next train out of town, that is."

Rush stared at her brother, wrinkled her nose, and frowned. "Well, hopefully she will follow us, now that she knows you're gone, too!"

"Hey, why didn't we just hop on a train? Maybe it would have got us to Idaho."

"That's what I mean, shut up. Just do as I say. Got it?"

"Yeah, yeah, yeah, I got it. No worries." Ryker laid back and put his front paws behind his head.

"I wish I had a baby bottle right now. I'd stick it right in your mouth. Or a pacifier!"

"Just make sure it's chocolate milk. Two percent, I don't like that other stuff." Ryker broke into a loud laugh.

"Shhhh… Please, Ryker, c'mon. Be quiet, at least. Take a nap or something, but zip it."

"Okay, Sis. Eyes are closed. I'm dreamin' now of your Utopian city with the 'cabbage grass green as Emeralds'," he blurted out sarcastically, quoting what he'd read. "Hey, I thought cabbage wasn't that good for us rabbits." Rush somehow kept her composure and simply rolled her eyes.

A thousand miles and three rest stops later, Rush and Ryker were staring at the Rocky Mountains, after jumping off the back of a small flatbed at a gas station outside Denver.

"C'mon, Ryker," Rush urged. "We've got to make it to Auntie Arlington's and see if she can help us find a way to Idaho."

"Man, look at those mountains. Wow! I'm gonna hop up one of those all the way to the top when I get older. You just watch and see!"

"Told you it was pretty out west. Feel that sunshine? I love it already!"

"Me too, Sis, right behind you. Just lettin' you lead for now." He picked up his pace, just a little, but still lagged behind.

Their aunt lived about three miles from the gas station, quite a ways to go. The Arlingtons were elderly hares but still had a lot of pep left in them and zest for life, especially since the frequency changes had occurred. Though older, Annie Arlington resembled her sister, had the same fluffy, mostly tan-colored fur, but her ears had begun sagging a bit and with all her nutritious but hearty eating habits and less exercise, both her and Harvey were a little pudgy at this time in their lives. Her husband was still handsome but his fur had turned completely grey.

The runaways hopped to it, hiking their little tails off. With the Colorado sunshine on their fur and the dry summer breeze at their backs, the two wanderers felt happy-go-lucky and absolutely sure of themselves. Hearts couldn't thump any harder than for two determined hares on a quest for a better life.

As they hopped along, Ryker prodded his sister, "Hey, Sis, what does love feel like? I mean you love this guy, Wrigley, huh? Just like Mom and Dad loved each other. Why didn't he want to come out with you? I mean if he loves you, he'd want to protect you and…"

"Oh shut up. I suppose you followed me over there, too. It's my personal business. And besides, who says I love him? Wrigley's got a lot of changing to do before I give my love to him!" She hopped along even faster trying to get away from her brother. But he stuck right behind her.

"Yeah sure, Sis. Whatever you say, Sis. Want some Kleenex to wipe your tears away? Here." Ryker ran around in front of her and handed his distressed sister a few tissues he had dug out from the front pouch of his backpack.

She took them. "Thanks. Now just keep moving, don't talk, okay? My little chaperone. Protector. I do see a lot of dad in you." She wiped a few more tears away and kept hopping. That made Ryker feel the best he'd felt in a long time. He smiled and felt so strong, like a true knight in shining armor.

"Hey, Sis, I see a lot of you in me, too. That's what Mom says, that we could just about be twins if we were the same age, we look so much alike."

"Don't push it. I'm me, and you are you. That's it. Just hop. Okay?"

"Sure, Sis, sure. I'm hoppin' and boppin' right with ya." Ryker laughed.

When they got there, Rush pleaded with her aunt NOT to call the Denver Rabbit Patrol. Her aunt promised and reassured her, said she had already talked with her mom. "I guess your friend let her know you were headed for Denver first. She knew you'd stop by here, so she called me."

"You talked to Mom? Was she like furious-gonna-kill-me mad, or more a worried-and-hoped-Ryker-and-I-were-both-okay kind of mad?" Rush anxiously awaited her aunt's response.

"Oh, she was furious all right, and worried sick. She's not happy about any of this. What were you thinking, Rush Palmer, up and running off like that? Anyway, she's decided to come after you and said she'd talk it out with you when we all meet there in New Jack Rabbit City."

"Really, she's coming out, oh good!" Rush was relieved, mission accomplished. She just knew her mom would love their new town and life in Idaho. She gave her aunt a hug. "Wait, what do you mean *all* of us?"

"Well, I kind of promised your mom we'd tag along. Keep an eye out for you and your brother. We always planned to retire out west, somewhere further away from the city, anyway. Besides, we've been to Boise before. We know just what trains to take. Why don't you give your mom a quick call and let her know you're here and safe. There's a pen by the phone to push the numbers with."

"Thanks, Auntie." Rush hopped toward the phone. "Where's Uncle Harvey?"

"He's coming. He's just packing up a few more things."

There was no answer at the host family house of Brook Palmer's residence, so Rush figured her mom had already left, and told Ryker all about it. Soon, off the foursome went, on an adventure, hoping for happy, new beginnings.

RUSH CRUSH

Rush, Rush, my crush is on you.
Hey Rush, my crush is on you.
Rush, Rush, my crush is on you.
I love you, Rush, you love me too?

We'll be good together,
two lover valentines.
Tell me you love me,
say you'll be mine.

Rush, Rush, my crush is on you.
I love you, Rush, you love me too?
Rush, Rush, my crush is on you.
Hey Rush, you love me too?

We'll talk and laugh and bike and hike
and have so much fun.
We'll be the envy, be the envy,
be the envy of everyone.

Rush, Rush, my crush is on you.
I love you, Rush, you love me too?
You made me see better days.
With you I feel so good.
Changin' my ways, changin' my ways,
even gonna leave this hood.

Rush, Rush, my crush is on you.
I truly love you. I truly do.
I'll change, I'll grow.
I'll make you proud as can be.

If you'll just believe,
keep believing in me.
You'll see, you'll see.
Fairytales can come true.

You for me and me for YOU!
Rush, Rush, my crush is on you.
I love you, Rush, I really do.
Rush, Rush, my crush is on you.
Hey Rush, you love me too?

Rush, Rush, my crush is on you.
I love you, Rush, you love me too?
Rush, Rush, my crush is on you.
Hey Rush, you love me too?

Rush, Rush, my crush is on you.
I love you, Rush, I truly do.

Chapter Four: South-Siders' Big Plans

"Dice, c'mon, put those stupid dice away and listen to me, will ya?" Caponey shouted over the boombox playing in the alleyway, some Bruce Springsteen song. The music equipment was a little outdated, but the bargain buy was one of Dice's slick trade deals he was proud of.

"I heard ya before. I ain't kidnappin' no pretty momma and hauling her furry tail all the way out to Boise just 'cause you believe in fairytales and funny magic water." Dice shook again and yelled, "C'mon, snake eyes!" as the dice hit the cardboard lying in the street, but all he got was a four and a two. He was a true gambler at heart, never beating the odds, but never giving up either. Not at the racetrack, not in his late-night poker games, nor on the streets of Chicago for that matter.

"Hey, Boss," Dice added, "That's a pretty darn lame idea anyway if you ask me. Maybe any rabbit or hare can just drink the water, don't need no kidnap barter scheme, if ya ask me. Wrigley ain't gonna like it much either, you hastlin' his girlfriend's momma."

"C'mon, Dice, I thought you was 'born to be wild.'" Dice ignored his remarks and kept throwing the dice.

The South-Siders lived in the alleyways of Chicago and spent a lot of time picking pockets, selling stolen goods, working their hotspot casino nights, and scamming gullible rabbits whenever they could. Oh, they had their big dreams, too, but most of them happened only at night when they finally fell asleep after another exhausting day of amateur gangsterism.

A few of them, like Meigs, Bronzey, Mugsey and Fuzzy, still kept hoping for some miracle sack of cash to fall from the sky, thinking that would solve all their problems. Maybe their gigs as The Rappin' Rabbits would really start hoppin', and they'd be rich and famous once and for all. Oh they knew they should really call themselves, The Rappin' Hares, but that just didn't sound as good, so they stuck with Rabbits and hoped nobody would notice the difference.

And, of course, Wrigley believed in his love for Rush, that it would somehow make everything okay, someday. Especially when he finally got to tell her the reason he stayed behind was to protect her mother.

The girls, blonde beauty Meigs and brainy brunette Bronzey, also held out hope that reading a story here or there from some of the romance novels they found in the alleyways after the Printers Row Lit Fest every year would make a knight in shining armor suddenly appear, and they'd live happily ever after. But those were fleeting thoughts for the gangster hares who began losing their way many years ago, due to one heartbreak or another. Nowadays it was all about survival, one day to the next.

Until one day, when Caponey overheard Wrigley and Rush talking about how dreams really could come true. All they had to do was make it to New Jack Rabbit City, drink the water, sprout up like *Jack in the Beanstalk*s, and then they could come back and rule the Southside as six-feet-tall kings. Even humans would have to deal with Caponey Ritso and the South-Siders, once and for all! He couldn't wait.

His reading and writing skills weren't that great. That's one of the reasons why he needed his buddy and the rest of the gang to accompany him on the trip out west. He didn't want to end up in New York or some other mistaken destination just because he couldn't read the signs. He was their leader, too. He couldn't give up that power, didn't want to either.

"Dice! Dice!" he yelled, getting the rabbit's attention. Mugsey and Fuzzy were busy telling a funny joke while waiting for Dice to roll again, and scowled at Caponey for interrupting.

Dice, the only rabbit in the gang of hares, stuck out like a sore spot, looking more like a Dalmatian puppy with his white and black fur. He wasn't supposed to get along with hares, but he sure did. Everyone liked Dice. Caponey offered him a free meal if he'd follow him over to Bourbon Street. After devouring the treat and listening to Caponey go on and on, Dice obliged his long-time partner in crime and conceded to follow what he thought was a half-bunny-brained idea: Kidnap this Rush girl's mom, high-hop it to Idaho, make darn sure they got their magic potion drink, become giants, and return to Chicago to rule.

Dice knew he gave in too easy at times to Caponey's big plans and gypsy-like whims, but he had his reasons. He figured his restless spirit needed some new adventures anyway. Not much for material things, except money, and the two large, but light-weight, cotton-square white and black-dotted dice he wore on a thin rope around his neck, it was easy for Dice to hit the road.

The rest of the gang, though, it took a lot of talking to convince them, especially Putzy. Caponey had a real tough time convincing him to pack up and leave behind some of his sentimental stuff, and stared down Putz, who didn't want to leave his garbage can.

"I says pack up your things, we're movin' out," he ordered again in his husky voice. Where the huskiness came from, nobody knew. Caponey always talked big, but wasn't much taller than the rest of the South-Siders, except Putz, who was just a petite, sweet-hearted nothing fancy all black English hare himself. "C'mon, get packin', Putz, don't ya wanna grow bigger? And we need to get movin' 'cause Wrigley's girl's got a head start on us."

"Ah jeez, you're listening to fairytale baloney stuff again. C'mon, we're s'posed to be Chicago gangsters, not rural bunnies hoppin' around in some crazy rabbit town in Idaho." Putz kept tinkering with the garbage can he'd found yesterday in the alleyway. He wanted to paint it up and put a little mattress in it. It was always difficult for Putzy to up and move, even if it meant just hopping over to a different dark alleyway, let alone a new state.

"What I say, we do. You know that. It's the way it's always been." Caponey slicked his ears back with his right paw, got some hair grease on it, and licked it off.

"Fire engine red. Man I love this color! Look, Boss, almost done." He looked up at Caponey, who was right in his face. Caponey thought that's all it would take, but he was wrong. It took another half hour of brooding and silence before Putz reconsidered – and only because he'd be left all alone, since all the other South-Siders were leaving.

When Caponey checked back on him, Putz finally gave in. "All right, all right already, I'm packin." He picked up the red backpack and went to go get his stuff. "Hey, Boss, this ain't gonna be big enough to get all my stuff in here, no way," Putz whined.

"You got so much junk, Putz. Pick and choose. One backpack's all you can handle carrying. You know that. Me? I got me my old suitcase. ONE suitcase here. Oh, and my lucky tie here, passed down and preserved for generations for the leader of the gang. Legend tells the story about how the real live human Caponey wore it during one of his arrests."

"Boss, I've heard that story so many times. I know, I know, okay. Your tie's the real deal," Putz lamented.

"Yeah, and *I'm* the real deal, the leader of this here gang, that'd be me! And you, Dice, and the rest of yous, you're all I got for family, and we're all you got. So go get rid of some of that junk of yours!" Caponey ordered loudly once again.

"Ah jeez." Putz moped on over to his bungalow to say goodbye to some of his belongings, things he sure would miss tinkering with. "I'll probly only find cabbage grass and sand out there, maybe creepy, crawlin' creatures of the desert—no tools, no cans, no nothin'," he mumbled to himself.

Soon, Caponey's plan was in action. After all, the South-Siders were family, they stuck together. So the gang of eight packed up and hopped on over to the Gold Coast to pick up their cargo insurance, a mom who was terrified because her daughter and son were runaways. The only South-Sider who didn't realize this was a stupid, lame, unnecessary kidnapping plan was, of course, Caponey. Wrigley tried to talk some sense into him. They all tried, but to no avail. The boss had it in his not-so-bright head that, just in case the giant rabbit he'd been hearing about wouldn't hand over the magic water easily, trading an innocent, motherly hare hostage would do the trick.

Chapter Five: Caponey's Unnecessary Hostage

While Caponey and the South-Siders were packing, so was Brooklyn Palmer. She had her mind made up, knew right from the start she couldn't just sit around and wait. After talking to Sheddy, she felt it was best to leave the Rabbit Patrol out of it, just go and retrieve the kids herself. All she had to do was make it out west somehow and talk some sense into her stubborn, misguided kids, and get them to return home.

After the phone call from her older half-sister, Annie in Denver, Mrs. Palmer felt some relief.   At least the kids had made it there safely.   Annie Arlington mentioned that she could call the Denver Rabbit Patrol, but again, Mrs. Palmer thought it best to handle it in her own way. Otherwise, Rush would probably never forgive her.

The last thing she packed up was a small photo in a frame of her, Ryker and Rush taken two years ago in front of The Buckingham Palace. Why do kids have to grow up? she wondered, sobbing. The plan was for a friend to drive her to the South Shore train, but that never happened.

She woke up foggy and unable to focus, with some strange scent filling her nostrils and sinuses. Then Mrs. Palmer heard voices, loud, mischievous laughter, and snoring. What kind of nightmare was this? "Ryker, Rush, kids, where are you?" she yelled out. Finally, after rubbing her eyes raw, she saw someone in front of her.

"What, who are you?" she stammered.

"Hush now, little hare. Don't fret. Caponey, at your service," he teased. "We'll be in Idaho in no time and you can be reunited with your kids. How's that for helping out a pretty momma who's lost her kids? Hey, Bronzey, get the little lady some water, will ya?"

"Yeah sure, no problem. Might as well keep your precious, silly cargo happy." Bronzey walked closer to Mrs. Palmer and sneered, "Anything else I can get you, ma'am, while you're traveling with us?"

Mrs. Palmer was too confused to pick up on the sarcasm. She smacked her lips and moved her tongue around in circles. "Maybe I could use that water, if you don't mind. My mouth is so dry."

"Yeah, sure. Like I said, no problem." Bronzey poured some water out from a jug into a small cup and handed it to the kidnapped victim.

"Thank you." She struggled with tied paws to hold the cup and gobbled down the water.

"Mugsey, Meigs, Fuzzy, Dice, c'mon over and say hello to our guest. She's awake now."

"Nah," said Dice, "we're good. Busy over here checking this next connection we gotta make."

Mrs. Palmer turned her head and looked all around the boxcar. Then she tried to rub her neck, but, of course, her hands were tied. "What's going on here? I demand to know right this very minute. Just what do you have in mind?" She stared into Caponey's glaring eyes.

"Well, ya see, it's like this, little lady. It's a win-win situation. We take you to get your kids back. Oh yeah, by the way, you should know that Wrigley has kind of a thing for your high-class daughter, Rush. That's how we knew where she was headed. They're kind of buddy-buddy, just in case you didn't know it. We turn you over, get 'invited' to drink the Holy Grail-like water there, grow big and tall. The kids get their mom back, and we go back home to reign over all the baby bunnies, and ebberybody's happy." Caponey grinned from rabbit-ear to rabbit-ear.

"What are you talking about?" And did he just say *ebberybody*? she thought to herself.

"The little Miss Rush didn't tell you about the magic water, the artesian spring?"

"No. I just know what I read in the note she left me. Some kind of new city in Idaho where rabbits live. What about the water? And why are my paws tied? It's not like I'm going to jump off this freight train or beat all of you up. Untie me this minute!"

"No, no, not so fast. You're our lucky ticket to all our dreams comin' true. Can't have ya escapin'. Can't have that. So you just sit tight." He smiled at her again. "Oh, and the water. Let's just say that your kids might encounter some growing pains while they're out there in New Jack Rabbit City. Because, ya see, the water is gonna make 'em big. I mean real big. Ya drink it and grow like six-feet-tall. That's what I'm talkin' about!" He flopped down on the hay covering the floor of the train and put his head on a pillow made of rags. "Now I'm gonna get me some rest. You just hang tight, little lady. You'll see, everything'll work out okay. We're not here to hurt anyone, just makin' dreams come true for ebberybody."

Caponey never could get that word right. And pillow, he always says pellow. It drives his gang members nuts. The others continued to ignore Mrs. Palmer and worked out the details of getting to New Jack Rabbit City. They knew they'd have to do the real planning. Caponey was good for the big scheme ideas, lame ones especially, but the details, he always needed help with those. Kidnapped, worried, and scary thoughts of her kids being six-feet-tall—that was Mrs. Palmer's reality for now. She hoped and prayed it would all change soon, and that her kids were safe. She couldn't hold back the tears. Not all bad, Meigs handed her a couple tissues, another cup of water, and a few cloverleaves.

"Thank you," the grateful captive said as Meigs walked back to join the others, where Caponey slept like a baby. Mrs. Palmer closed her eyes and tried to think of a way out of her frightening dilemma. At least she was going to see her kids.

Chapter Six: Magical Moments and Secrets

"You're underfoot," Abby said, a bit agitated at Zach as she pushed a right hand between his shoulder blades. "Spread out!" The dogs lengthened their stride to the right and left of us. Past the city limits sign, the terrain did not vary. Still no signs of jacks. Climbing a small dune, we reached the top, and then my jaw dropped! Here, hidden in a small valley was an array of platforms, ramps, stilts, all tucked into the bitterbrush. My first appraisal was that it was some sort of obstacle course, and I muttered aloud, "Is this where they train?"

Should I expect to see cutouts of dogs, coyotes, hawks? Do they dodge and bolt through and between these strange structures? Do they familiarize rabbit recruits with some kind of tactical movement here? Where were they? The dogs turned their sandy noses skyward, sucking air and snorting, their nostrils filtering the air for scents, but nothing. All these questions and still there were no answers. I looked to Abby to fill in the blanks, if she could.

"Looks like lumber scrounged from the local farms. Most of it's picnic table tops, must have come from the park," she said.

Can these jacks be carpenters, too? I mused. The structures were crudely built, but pretty cool. I could only imagine rabbits running on top of these planks, ducking and hiding from imaginary predators, perhaps real ones, at their broad-footed heels. Some of the eerie planks silhouetted the sky. There seemed to be purpose to it all. They probably learned and practiced their skills here, how to evade any threats to capture – in essence, how to survive. Through this run of what reminded me of fish skeletons, we reached a stand of trees, if you could call two hemlock trees a stand. And there, braced against the tallest of the hemlocks, stood a figure with his other arm leaning against his hip.

"Meet the Mayor of New Jack Rabbit City," Abby said without hesitation.

It was magical, this moment: the last step before turning back, the dawn that's always rising, the sun that never sets. A spin of reality, the glimpse of what can be—a tunnel into the open mind.

What about the dogs? Would they rip into this six-foot creature, would I witness the greatest dog and rabbit fight of all time? It never happened. Much to my surprise, the dogs walked up to this lanky jack, and with a calming hand, he stroked them both. Eggy responded with a wag of the tail and Nasty did the same. Here, leaning against the hemlock tree, its branches spanning the sky, just a hundred feet away, quite calm and steady, this jackrabbit was petting my dogs.

He was dressed rather oddly. I guess any clothed rabbit would seem odd, though. His apparel was a 1950's picnic style. His shoes, most notable, resembled stitched, checkered tablecloths, tailored quite smartly into high-top, ballooned-out, Bozo the Clown footwear. The shirt and tie, probably fashioned from a bed sheet, I guessed, perhaps from some local farm refuse. Still, for all my scrutiny, he appeared well-dressed. His hat bore the crest of a rabbit holding a small heart with an arrow running through it, a Cupid connotation, I surmised.

Abby was the first to speak. "So we meet again, your Honorable Mayor."

The jack stepped forward, paused one more time to run an eye over me and said, "So it is."

It is this moment I will never fail to remember, me standing before a dune, in scrub brush, on a late spring afternoon, a giant rabbit positioned right in front of me, speaking perfect English. The powwow commenced. I would say we sat around on a log but, in this stark landscape, seating was cross-legged on the sand. The canopy above us was merely the lone hemlock tree with just branches, black silhouettes against the blue sky.

"I remember our first meeting," Abby said. "It was late fall, two years ago, a day I'll never forget. I reached the top of a small dune and there you were."

The rabbit responded with a nod of the head. "I could have disappeared in a twinkle of your eye, but I'd spent time watching you. We watch everyone who enters the city limits. Most pass through, never noticing our rabbit housing, but you were different, wide-eyed. I knew you were a dreamer. You gotta look past the sage, sand, burning sun to see the beauty here, as we see it."

"I was six then and very young, now I'm eight and I guess a little smarter. Thanks for visiting with me again. I brought my brother, Zach, with me this time, and my Uncle Mike. He has the two dogs, Eggy and Nasty."

It was just now that I glanced over at Zach. In my own amazement, I'd forgotten about him. He had taken a seat on the ground to my right. The twelve-year-old, with a wide-eyed gaze, followed every move of the Mayor. He looked hypnotized, which is the way I felt.

I finally spoke up, but the words caught in my throat, "How can this be?"

The Mayor of New Jack Rabbit City became like a keynote speaker up on a podium. "Let me tell you. We are backcountry people," he said, slowly and carefully.

"People" – interesting word to use, I thought. The words that came into my mind were "tribe" or "clan," maybe "creatures," but *people*?

"We are not cottontails or bunnies. We are rabbits!" These words rumbled out of his belly. "Deep in this outback, here in Idaho, we live. A land too tough to cultivate, too remote, and avoided by all but the crazies. My people are from the Owyhee breaks, where the sins of Nevada try to crawl in bed with self-righteous folks of Idaho." Did this rabbit have a political agenda, too? I smiled to myself, my comfort level rising.

The Mayor drawled on. "Range fires, drought, and man brought us here to the park. Our needs are few. The desires of my people are much like yours, peace and families, but our family of rabbits is unlike any others. So much happened in such a short time. I can see from your amazement that you have not seen a rabbit like me, this large and so similar to you. We, of course, were not always like this, nor do all of us appear in this manner. I tell you quite honestly, it still startles me when I look into the mirror of a pool of water and see this figure now standing before you. There were two events that changed our lives forever here: the discovery of the artesian spring, and the new digital frequency."

IT'S
THE FREQUENCY

His brief history of New Jack Rabbit City held my rapt attention, but his last words, the "artesian spring and the new digital frequency," dropped my jaw. I glanced over to Abby and Zach to see if these words almost stopped their breathing as it did mine. They both looked up at me at the same time wondering if I could explain all of the unbelievable information the Mayor was sharing. I simply shrugged my shoulders and wondered: Will he share more details? Were we to become like *The Raiders of the Lost Ark*? The tall talking rabbit loosened his droopy tie and started up a small hill.

I assumed his lead was an invitation to follow. The three of us brushed the sand off our bottoms and continued to exchange looks of excitement. The dogs, Eggy and Nasty, shook their tails in anticipation for the guidance. But what surprised me most was the lack of any fear. Here we were, in this *Ripley's Believe It or Not* moment, and we all followed him with determination. I played his words over and over again in my head as we marched across the sand like ants, two kids, two dogs, and me.

Dwarfed in this huge landscape, we headed to a place we could only have imagined, and we got a much more vivid picture as the

Mayor filled us in and our eyes took it all in, more of the magical wonderland.

"Here it is, New Jack Rabbit City: fifty acres of land, a four-hundred seventy-foot sand dune, two lakes, and three spring-fed streams. This natural sand trap is made from a web of brush, vine, and tree isles. The vegetation spirals like ridges of a person's fingerprints and gives the impression of a maze to the uninvited. The black and silver sagebrush, rabbit brush, antelope bitterbrush, and purple sage entangle these islands."

"Wow!" Zach exclaimed. Abby and I just stood there quietly, mesmerized by what we saw.

"Trees: water birch, hemlock (my favorite), and hawthorne brace the vines and tumbleweeds to form impassable walls in this flora and fauna fortress. The residents here, my fellow rabbits and hares, know of secret passages into these islands where areas as big as football fields can be hidden from view. Actually, we can maintain one hundred percent visibility and/or invisibility whenever we choose. Often it is within hidden neighborhoods that our lives go on daily here. But there are days when all can be seen with human eyes. It is certainly at our choosing, however."

As the Mayor glided down a small hill, he added, "Now let's move on so I can tell you about the secret life of water. Most folks take it for

granted. You have your lakes, rivers, and taps, turn a lever and it pours. In this desert, when it pours, a pool appears and then disappears right before your eyes. It is the *knowledge* of water that keeps us alive here. It can be fierce or gentle and hidden in places you would never think to look. Without it, this would all be dust and sand in your shoes."

Abby, quiet with awe, said, "It all seems so tame here."

"It is," the Mayor responded, "but historically and geographically, where all of our ancestors came from, it was quite different." He stood upright, a full six-feet-tall or more, and gazed off into the distance. His long ears bobbed right, then left. "Downpours split the gulches open, drowned even the strongest rabbit, or whatever got caught in its torrent. It still does sometimes. Look to the horizon, the irrigators spray water everywhere, the land turns green but the desert always pushes back."

The bigger-than-life rabbit paused; then pushed through some low branches, and an odd building appeared in the distance. "There's the springhouse. Follow me."

We kept moving. Abby still shadowed the Mayor. I am not sure, but at times I think I heard whispers between the two. The dogs now thirsted for water and I reached for a bottle strapped to my belt. I handed it to Zach, who drank, but Abby and the Mayor stayed out of reach. The wind went silent as we moved through hollow and bitterbrush. The horizon swayed in front of my fatigued eyes.

Suddenly, a loud humming sound came to life, a tremor from the ground that stirred the air around our faces. It seemed like some kind of murmur dancing in space. Eggy's ears stiffened to attention; Nasty's head twitched. The dogs froze, pupils widened and their paws now stood on moist ground. Was it a mirage? Water poured out of the earth. Seconds later their tongues splashed and gulped the flowing water. They languished in this rhapsody of blue. Abby, Zach and I peered into the spring. It bubbled up and out of nowhere, rippled, pooled, and a flood of blue like a Persian rug lay out on the desert floor. And then it was gone. No tailing stream, just a solid current right down a hole.

"This artesian spring created the rabbit you're looking at right now," the Mayor said. "This land is our home. We know every bush and bramble. It just started percolating up, right before our eyes. Ten years ago, I was the first to drink from it, and the change was dramatic. I went from a good-sized jack to the tall rabbit you see right now, not overnight but darned near. Many drank and the results were often the same. Although we're large, we blend like sunlight into the landscape, invisible if we want to be." He paused for just a moment and took a deep breath. "Even our body temperatures adapted, so during hot or cold weather, we are always comfortable. Then our size, city, and our lives took another monumental turn when they changed the frequency. It was the frequency that put this shirt on my back and these words in my mouth. It was then that we tuned in!"

The Mayor's ears pointed up like a church steeple. "There's the Santa Fe freight train. It will stop at the switchyard near New Jack Rabbit City, then move on to Mountain Home."

Zach cocked his head, looked north toward Mountain Home, and said, "I don't hear anything, do you, Uncle Mike?"

With my ears stretching into the silence, I said, "Even with a set of ears like his, I doubt if I could hear a noisy sugar beet truck out on Old State Road 78."

We hiked along a trail of sand, a serpent's back, until we reached the springhouse. The large corrugated steel building sat in a tiny clearing, with a small silo at one end. It looked like a launching pad. The hum of water pouring out onto some smooth surface rattled the air. We stopped, and following the lead of this six-feet-tall jackrabbit, we took a seat on the green grass, real grass, in this world of sun-bleached sand.

"Enjoy this oasis. This is one of the many secrets we have in our city. You could walk right past one and not even know it was there. We take pride in all of our common areas and a special pride in hiding them from most curious travelers – except a special few, like you." He laughed as we all smiled at him. "Someday, I'll take you on a tour of our business district. You can see our production lines of: clothing, electronics, and healthy foods. We are always growing, but right now we have a block long section of town, kind of like one of your Mini-Mall places where residents can hop or walk in and trade for products. No money exchanges, we simply use your old-fashioned barter system which works remarkably well." The Mayor paused and watched our excited reactions.

"Now, let me get back to the frequency change. Yes indeed, June 12th, 2009 is a day few humans remember, but we will certainly never forget it."

I glanced over to Abby and Zach to see if a light bulb had lit in their eyes. The wheels were still turning. Abby was speechless, for once. I looked down at Eggy and Nasty. With their eyes closed, they were enjoying the comfort of the grass and snoring.

"It was official that day, but the testing had gone on for years."

"Testing," "official," this still did not ring a bell.

"Rabbits are wired like no other animal," he continued. "Our ears are most sensitive, a two-antennae-array constantly monitoring our surroundings. That train I just heard is nine miles north of here. The footsteps climbing the big dune, I can hear them now, as clearly as you hear my voice."

At this point he raised a paw and stroked his left ear. "We could always hear static, a weak pulse, a frequency vibrating in the vast cyberspace. Images began to appear, voices, scenes from strange places; we all saw visions flash before our eyes that weren't really there. It was frightening at first, but we learned to ride the frequency. We tuned in, caught on. See, our brains have four frontal lobes, twice as many as you humans. These extra lobes quickly processed the signals and within months we were up to speed with the human race. We mimicked you at first but then true thinking and reasoning began. We reached total mental superiority over all the animals around us, and I bet we can put up a pretty good debate with most humans."

The Mayor's face went blank, as if he could look through a hole in space. "The news just started on the Fox network."

Chapter Seven: The Arrival

Huddled inside boxcars of the Santa Fe freight train chugging closer to Mountain Town, Idaho, a motley crew of dreamy rabbits couldn't wait to jump off and head for New Jack Rabbit City, their new home. The Buckinghams, in a front car, were the first to get ready. Rush, Ryker, and their aunt and uncle, the Arlingtons, had connected with the same freight train and had gotten comfortable in another boxcar closer to the caboose. The South-Siders would be catching up with them within a few hours.

"Hear that whistle?" Mr. Buckingham shouted. "It means we're almost there, near New Jack Rabbit City." He was right. Wyndhameer could see parts of the switchyard now as the train slowed down.

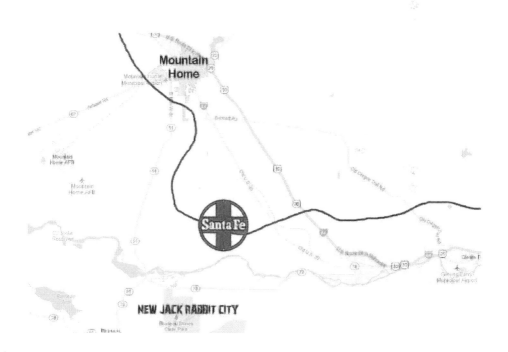

"There is so much history to be recalled at the crossroads here near Mountain Home, Idaho. They say, back in the olden days, Billy the Kid, Jesse James, and many other well-known outlaws passed through this territory," he informed his wife and son. Bobbiteer, especially, loved history and reading about outlaws, and sometimes pretended to be a notorious character.

The tracks of the rail yard were laid out like centipede skeletons in the sun-baked sand. Six tracks appeared maintained and active; four lie dormant, overrun with tumbleweeds, sagebrush, and sand where they weren't protected from the occasionally relentless winds. Old freight cars sat parked on the rusted rails, with doors open and spilling cardboard stapled to splitting palettes.

Cattle cars lined miles of rails with the next passengers, fattened cows from the feedlots, the same lots the hares had seen other cows dotting the neighborhood hills today, as they got closer to arrival. The belting chorus of moos meant Bobbiteer had to shout to be heard.

"Listen to the cows! Hey, look at those wild-colored cars!" He pointed to some cars that were spray-painted with bold colors: red, purple, blue, green and yellow. "I can make out some words. Maybe it's some kind of secret message from the big rabbits," Bobbiteer speculated.

"Yes, or some senseless act from some undisciplined kids," Wyndhameer suggested. He noticed how the graffiti contrasted with the more neutral, earthy shades of the desert landscape. Three tracks over, active cars were sitting on steel wheels. Two railroad workers were coupling those cars with a hundred or more other cars. Probably designated for the next trip across America, or at least some states, Wyndhameer thought to himself.

Bobbiteer was excited, but of course he was still the only one who hated the idea of leaving Chicago and his friends behind. The rest, even Mr. and Mrs. Arlington, knew a whole new adventure awaited them. They were actually planning on moving to Arizona until Rush came along with all of her dreams and aspirations for a more serene, rural lifestyle in Idaho.

Wyndhameer and Miranda felt like they had done their job as good parents, packing up and getting Bobbiteer out of that big city chaos, before it was too late. They both had a profound feeling that everything, simply everything in their lives, would be better, more wholesome and adventurous, safer and healthier than ever before.

"Well, Miranda, we did it, sweetheart," Wyndhameer said proudly, hugging his wife.

"Yes, dear. I'm so happy you talked me into this. It's so beautiful! I can't wait to see the town and meet the Mayor." A few tears fell onto her furry cheekbone.

"Now, Miranda, one thing. Just because I hear this Mayor dresses fancy and stands six-feet-tall, please don't expect me to start changing everything about me, okay? Promise me." He stood up and hoisted their backpacks onto his shoulders.

"Who, me? I wouldn't change a thing, not a thing," she professed, wiggling her nose, which made her whiskers flog up and down.

"Son, grab your backpack, this is it. The train's at a full stop. Now's the time. Not sure how far we'll have to hop, but I don't think it's too far. We'll stop and ask the first hare family we see. I hope there are some still living outside of N.J.R.C."

"Okay, Dad, I'm ready. Hey, you think you could write Beatledoo's dad and mom a letter whenever we get settled? Maybe you can talk them into coming out west, too. Please?" Bobbiteer pleaded as he stood near the opening of the boxcar ready to jump.

"Sure, Son. Let's see what we've got here; then maybe your mom could do that for you. She's better at that kind of stuff than me. Okay, on the count of three, are you ready?" Wyndhameer coaxed.

"Ready!" Bobbiteer and Miranda answered simultaneously.

"One, two, THREE. JUMP!"

While the Buckinghams hopped off toward their new adventurous lives, Rush and Ryker, who loved the train ride, knew it was time to get ready to jump off, so they gathered up their backpacks. Their Auntie and Uncle Arlington were following right behind a teenager's whims.

"Harvey, you're not afraid to jump, are you?" Annie Arlington worried about her husband because he had a bad right knee. Sometimes it hurt, sometimes it didn't.

"Oh, Annie, you know me. You didn't forget my skydiving adventure already, did you? If I could do that in my old age, I think I've got this dear. Shoot, if that frequency would have kicked in when I was a youngster, you'd probably be married to a parachute soldier from the 82nd Airborne, like old man Georgie, our human neighbor, who lived down the block from us," he boasted confidently as he stood at the edge of the boxcar door opening right alongside Rush and Ryker.

Annie Arlington still worried. "Now, Rush, Ryker, you be careful. We're right behind you. Okay?"

"Yes, Auntie Annie. We'll be careful. Right, Ryker?"

"Yeah, Sis. I promise, Auntie Annie, Uncle Harvey, we'll be careful. You, too. Hey, Sis, you think I can get a job here, instead of going to school? Dad always said I'm the boss, the head of the family."

Rush knew very well that Ryker would do anything he could to get out of going to school. "He never said *boss*. What Dad said was that you were the *man* of the house, soggy carrot-stick brain. And you know he'd want you to finish school and no way is Mom going to let you out of that! Now, are you ready to jump?"

"Yeah, yeah, I'm ready. And Dad never said you were the boss either, but you sure are bossy." He frowned and kicked a rock right off the train that almost hit a big black and white Collie who happened to be strolling by. "Hey, Sis, look, a cute doggy, maybe we could take him to New Jack Rabbit City with us."

"Nah, better leave him be. He might be one of those herd dogs I read about. Strange, he's just trotting along near this train. He's probably headed back to his job or some nice family, or he's waiting for someone. Okay, ready? On the count of three. One, two, THREE JUMP!" The brother and sister team jumped off, rolled for a ways, came to a stop, stood up, and brushed the dirt off their fur.

Annie looked at her husband's face and saw a scared old rabbit, not a soldier ready to jump out of an airplane. She noticed his grip getting stronger and stronger as Annie counted away for him.

Harvey felt relieved after the jump but ached as he stood up. He hid his pain from his wife, though. "Pretty good jump for an old guy and little gal like yourself," he said as he grinned from rabbit-ear-to-rabbit-ear.

Mrs. Arlington dusted her fur off. "Are you sure you're okay, Harvey?"

"Fit as a parachuting soldier after a clear landing," he assured her.

"You sure you guys are okay?" Rush asked, directing her concern toward her uncle and aunt.

"Looks like we're fine, dear. We're ready to hop alongside of you."

"Now what? Which way, Sis?"

"Hmm. Not sure, Ryker. Give me a minute."

"Not sure? Jeez, that's why you need a bodyguard around. See that? There goes some rabbits right there with backpacks. Just *wonder* where they are headed," Ryker teased his sister.

"Oh shut up. But good observation. C'mon, let's follow them."

"Okay, but I'm leading. You might get lost and have to call for your mommy or something." Ryker broke into a loud laugh.

"Oh my gosh. Why? Why me? Just lead, go ahead and lead you bright, bratty brother." And they hopped onward toward their dreams.

The Arlingtons just looked at each other and smiled. They were used to the contentious relationship their niece and nephew had.

As far as dreams, Rush wanted a better life for her mom. Hoped she really was coming out to look for them. Her mom would see how much happier she'd be living away from the big city and not working herself to death.

All Ryker ever wanted was to be just like his dad, a good guy and protector. Well, maybe that and a Karate champion. The Arlingtons, they simply wanted to enjoy each new day and grow older together. As they all hopped on feeling wild and free, the Idaho sunshine and soft breezes welcomed them.

Chapter Eight: Chicago Hares Meet

"Now stick close, you kids," Uncle Harvey cautioned. "You can't ever figure who hangs around freight yards like this. And stay clear from the train, it looks like it's getting ready to roll again."

"Yeah, stay close, Rush," Ryker mimicked.

Rush rolled her eyes and poked him in the back with her front paw. He took it in stride since he knew he deserved it, except that it made his backpack slip off and fall to the ground, so he fell behind a few steps.

"Kid! Kid! Hey, c'mere." Ryker looked to his right and saw a wild, scroungy-looking tall black-and-white rabbit, who peeked out between two of the freight cars.

"What? Who are you?" Ryker asked wide-eyed and curious.

"Wiley. Wiley Whiskers. I rule around these here parts. Hey, let me trade you a human-made, crisp, new twenty dollar bill for that backpack of yours. Whaddaya say? You look like a smart kid, know a good deal when you see one." Wiley grinned.

"I don't know. I kinda need my…"

"Ryker!" Rush looked back and shouted. "Get over here right this minute."

"Sorry, I gotta go. My sister thinks she's the boss of me, but it's really the other way around. Bye." He hoisted his backpack onto his left shoulder and marched forward.

"Well, you know where to find me, kid, if you want a good deal. Just come and see 'ol Wiley Whiskers." He had to shout out the last few words as Ryker faded away.

"Did you forget everything Mom and Dad taught you about talking to and trusting strangers?" Rush asked.

"I wasn't talking, he was. So there, Miss Bossy!" He stuck out his tongue.

"C'mon you two. Looks like someone's up this way, let's ask directions," Auntie Arlington said.

Harvey directed his inquiry to the family of rabbits standing before him, a couple with their young son: "Excuse me, do you happen to know the way to New Jack Rabbit City?"

"Well, to tell you the truth, sir, we're looking for the same. Hello, my name is Wyndhameer Buckingham. This is my wife, Miranda, and my son, Bobbiteer."

"Hello. A pleasure." The two shook paws. "My name is Harvey Arlington. This is my dear wife, Annie, and my niece and nephew, Rush and Ryker." Everyone gave each other a nod, and Bobbiteer and Ryker couldn't help staring at each other, wondering if they were meeting up with a cool kid or a nerd.

After disclosing that, strangely enough, all were newcomers to Idaho from the same hometown of Chicago, they found a local rabbit, named Bruno, who worked at the switchyard and got some directions for their destination. The local gave more than just directions though. He told the transient visitors that they might not find what they're looking for.

"That story about a Mayor, fancy new town and six-feet-tall rabbits, it just ain't so. Least-wise, ain't none of us seen it. Don't see any of us locals standin' six feet up in the air, do ya?" He took a puff off of a fat cigar. "But you can march along that way." He pointed. "Just keep heading out until you see the beach and a sign that reads: *New Jack Rabbit City*. Maybe your eyes will see the invisible, who knows." Bruno took another puff and blew the smoke right into Harvey Arlington's face.

After coughing a few times, Harvey said, "Well, much obliged. Thank you for your time."

That was it. The Arlingtons, Buckinghams, and Rush and Ryker were headed for their dream town. They only walked about half a mile, though, before they all sat down and had some lunch. With water jugs filled at the switchyard, they quenched their thirst and enjoyed a picnic lunch of carrots, hay, and celery. All energized after their meal, they hiked on until Bobbiteer was the first one to spot the sign.

"Hey, there it is, Dad, the sign, we must be here!" He looked over to Ryker. "My dad says I'm gonna grow really big here."

"Yeah, well if you do, I'm gonna get big, too," Ryker said matter-of-factly, wishing with all his heart his dad was standing next to him as well. "I don't see anybody, do you, Rush?"

"No. Nothing. Just this beach and sand. Should we keep going, Uncle Harvey?"

The adults all looked at each other for a definitive answer. Mr. Buckingham finally said, "I say we keep going. C'mon," and he began to lead the way.

As they hiked along, suddenly all the rabbits, young and old, experienced a ringing in their ears and a pounding in their heads. The oldest couple, the Arlingtons, got dizzy and had to sit down.

"What is that?" Harvey and Annie wiped the perspiration from their foreheads and rubbed their temples.

"Whoa! I hear clicking," said Bobbiteer to Ryker. "Do you hear it?"

"Wow! Yeah, wow! It's like radio station channels changing, clicking from one to another. Rush, Sis, you hear it, too?" He turned to his sister, who was shaking her head and scratching at her ears.

"Uncle Harvey, what's going on? Auntie Annie, help!" Rush fainted and fell to the ground.

While still rubbing their ears and blinking their eyes, everyone focused on helping Rush. As they surrounded her, fanned at her head and splashed some water on her face, a deep voice from over by a tree said, "Leave her. She'll be fine in just a little time. It's the frequency, you're all tuning in. Let it be and you'll be all right." The voice from behind the tree sounded so reassuring.

IT'S THE FREQUENCY

Seconds later, the visiting rabbits all got their first look at a true six-feet-tall rabbit. As he stepped out from behind the hemlock tree, the Mayor tipped his hat and said, again in a reassuring voice, "Welcome to New Jack Rabbit City. Don't worry. It's your antennae fine-tuning. The discomfort will soon pass and you'll be fine. Not only fine," he laughed loudly, "but tuned in like never before."

Wyndhameer and Miranda knew in an instant that New Jack Rabbit City was the real thing and they'd made the right decision in uprooting their son to this incredible land of opportunity. Not only could they grow big if they wanted so they could protect themselves better, but they would probably become even more intelligent, enhancing the quality of their lives.

Miranda stared at her husband and son – she could see the dramatic effects the frequency was having on them, on all of them. Their ears perked up straighter than ever, their eyes appeared more alert, and they just seemed more attentive to their surroundings.

The Mayor of New Rabbit City knew that they'd need some time to adjust. He stood by the tree and watched over them, standing by if he was needed. Within a half-hour, the transformation was complete.

"Like I said, welcome to New Jack Rabbit City." He laughed loudly again and smiled.

Welcome to
New Jack Rabbit
City
CITY LIMIT
POP. 367

Chapter Nine: The Olden Days

The South-Siders made good time and arrived only a few hours behind the other Chicago Hares. It took one initial bumpy, squeaky train ride, two transfers to truckers going west, a two-mile-hike, and yet another train, but the gang of eight and their captive hostage finally made it to Idaho, very near New Jack Rabbit City.

The South-Siders managed to hop off the slow-moving train unscathed, just before the switchyard. Disaster struck, though, for Brooklyn Palmer. Caponey kept yelling at her to jump, but she was scared and just refused to do it. Wrigley stayed with her. He held her paw for the third time, counted to three and tried again. This time, though, Brooklyn pulled back right as he said "three." She slipped, but Wrigley was already in motion, and he had to let go. Mrs. Palmer tumbled forward and smacked down on some rocks, got all skinned up and twisted her right leg. Wrigley felt terrible. The other South-Siders had all hopped ahead and didn't even see what had happened. It wasn't easy for Mrs. Palmer, limping along to catch up with the others. She had to hang on to Wrigley for help, as much as she hated it.

Caponey put his old suitcase on the ground, plunked himself down under a shady bush, and dug out a small bottle of water.

"I say while we got us some shade we take a little snooze. What do you say ebberybody, all you South-Siders?"

"I don't know, Boss," Dice said, "I wanna see that Mayor, see if anything's for real here. Might get dark pretty soon, too. Maybe we should keep a movin' – what do you guys and gals think?"

But before they could answer Caponey hopped back up and gave a clear order. "I says we're takin' a break. Now park it! All yous!" He frowned at Dice. "I swear, Dice, what's gotten into you lately? All that thinkin' on your own since all them frequency changes, not so sure it's a good thing for you. Now wake me up in about an hour. Got it?" He tapped Dice on the back. "Thanks, buddy. You, all yous, get ya some rest."

Most of the South-Siders weren't sure why they put up with Caponey giving orders, but they did. For Dice, it was different; he knew why. He'd still be wasting away, probably dead, rotting in a cage in the back alleyways of Chicago, if it wasn't for Caponey setting him free one rainy night years ago. After everyone settled in to rest, Dice fiddled with the string holding the cotton dice around his neck; he had to get a knot out.

Bronzey and Meigs fooled with their fur and pulled out a couple of celebrity magazines. They were always wishing they were human, so they could run off to Hollywood and become movie stars. Sometimes, though, they thought about being back home.

"It's so beautiful here. Look at this place: all the sand, beautiful sky, bushes, trees. Caponey says there's a beach, too, or I wouldn't have come. Can't wait to see that. You don't see all this in Chicago alleyways. I feel like we're back in Indiana, out in the country, on our farm, because it's so quiet and peaceful. Hey, Meigs, you think we'll ever get back home?"

"I don't know, Bronzey. We always said we'd make it *big*. Maybe we'll grow big here or get famous and wanna go back. We'll see. Let's find a place to rest for now, what do ya say?"

"Sure, Sis. Sure."

Mugsey and Fuzzy, two grey frizzy-furred hares, always stuck together and they nodded off right away leaning against each other's shoulders. They claimed they were half brothers, but never could prove it.

Suddenly it was quiet. The desert had a calming effect on the Chicago hares and Dice. All of them were resting. Caponey fell into a deep sleep. He didn't know why he was back in Chicago, but he was. He began to move his lips, but he couldn't talk. All the other South-Siders, too, there was something terribly wrong. Nobody talked. They just kind of hopped around looking at each other, like in the olden days, before the frequency changed. Even the boombox Dice owned was nowhere to be seen. No music? No gamblin' going on, either, just civilized bunnies, rabbits, and hares hopping along in the alleyways of the windy city.

Caponey moaned and moaned. He shook his head from right to left, pawed violently at his ears and tried to tune in so he felt smarter, could think like humans and talk. Nothing. He kicked his feet, tossed, turned. Nothing.

Dice hopped right up to him and simply looked into Caponey's eyes. Again, Caponey tried to move his lips and talk but all he could do was wiggle his nose. Finally, words came: "This must be a dream. I wanna wake up! This is just a dream. I know it is. I know I can talk!" He started screaming it aloud.

"Boss! Boss! Wake up! Boss! I'm here. It's Dice. Your buddy, Dice. You okay, Boss?" He kept shaking him.

"Oh jeez, Dice. Dice, my man. What do we gotta have dreams for if it's all just nightmare stuff? Jeez, I couldn't move my lips or talk. None of yous either. I lost the frequency magic. I never wanna go back to that. We're smart now. Us hares and rabbits, we're all smart and we can talk. Just wait 'till we get six-feet-tall, too. Oh man! Forget those dreams. All yous, ebberybody," he shouted, "wake up! We gotta get movin'. We got some growin' to do!" He rubbed his lips and felt so lucky that once again words were coming out of his mouth. "A, B, C, D, E, F, G..." He rambled off the alphabet as fast as he could. All the South-Siders and Mrs. Palmer were up and ready to go. "Hey, what's the little lady doin' untied? Whose idea was that?"

"Ah, she isn't goin' anywhere, Boss," Wrigley stood up for her. "She just wants to find her kids. C'mon, let's go. I'll stick with her."

"All right, for now. But you better not let her out of your sight. Got it, lover boy? I know you're sweet on this Rush girl. Good luck South-Sider. Let's go."

Caponey started in one direction and Wrigley had to correct him, "It's that way, Boss, if we wanna find that beach sign." Just because the boss had a map didn't mean he knew how to read it.

Every one of the South-Siders noticed how calm and quiet it was in the desert, compared to the city. Back on the move, they soon found a deserted old shack and snuck in. They needed some more time to think and plan. Most of the gang felt as if Mrs. Palmer was an unnecessary nuisance, but they acted as if they were sorry she got hurt. Although when Caponey gave one of his orders – to tie up the hostage again – Mugsey followed through and tied up one of her paws to some steel pipes that were lying on the ground next to her. While they looked over the map to start planning, Caponey plunked down on some hay, used his backpack for a pillow, closed his eyes, and started snoring again. The other hares just laughed as they often did when the boss acted lazy or did something silly or stupid.

Wrigley got out the water and gave Mrs. Palmer some sips. Then he found some rags and kept apologizing as he tried to help Mrs. Palmer clean her leg wounds.

She pushed him away, though, saying she could do it herself. Taking three deep breaths, she tried her best to relax. It looked as if the mother and child reunion would have to wait a little while longer. "Just find my kids for me, okay?" Her bottom lip quivered.

Wrigley looked into her sad eyes. "Everything will work out," he whispered. "Don't worry. And Rush and Ryker are probably here already. Really, don't sweat it. Hang in there." He winked and started to hop away.

But Mrs. Palmer had a lot to say about all of the recent shenanigans. "You're just a bunch of hoodlums, aren't you? I suppose your mothers didn't love you like they should have. Is that it, Wrigley? But I've got to tell you, it seems like you might be the smartest, kindest of the bunch here. This six-feet-tall dream of yours— it's not gonna solve all your problems, even if it does happen. I'd say this Mayor, *if* he exists, would be much more likely to accommodate nice, kind rabbits, not gangsters who kidnap mothers. What do you think?" She stared right into his dark but keen eyes.

All Wrigley wanted to do was tell her how much he loved her daughter, but knew it was not the right time or place. "I know, I know. This is a half-brained idea of Caponey's. You seem like a nice hare and I know you gotta be a cool mom 'cause Rush told me how much she loves ya." He reached over to untie Mrs. Palmer. "Here, let me get that paw free, so you can drink some more water."

"Well, thank you Wrigley. See, I knew you were a smart hare. But listen here, if you think my daughter is going to take up with any kidnapper or South-Sider gangster hoodlum, you'd better just think again. I just won't have it." She rubbed her paw where the rope had been, then sipped some water, poured a little water on a cloth and dabbed at the scrapes on her leg. "But thank you for the water. And tell your 'boss' when he quits snoring and wakes up that I'm not going anywhere, so no need for me being tied up again. Okay? I'm here to find my daughter and son and I'm not leaving until I do!" She gave Wrigley one final scornful look. But then she couldn't help herself and she cracked a little smile and softened up her stare.

"Don't worry, Mrs. Palmer, we'll find her. And Ryker. Everything will turn out. But just so ya know, my mom *did* love me. Thing is, there's a raw deal called cancer. I only knew my mom when I was real little, but I'll never forget her. I don't know why I'm telling you this stuff. Just get some rest, will ya?" He shuffled a few yards away, plopped down, crossed his arms, closed his eyes and relived some happy times he remembered with his mom.

Mrs. Palmer remained silent. She knew the kid was hurting. Also felt as if there was hope for him. But her thoughts quickly turned to her own son and daughter. She looked up, "Please God, let them be all right. Please watch over my kids and Annie and Harvey."

Chapter Ten: The Big Frequency Change

When the kids and I saw the Mayor again, he told us even more about all the big changes. So this was it, the change from analog to digital television, and I thought about the converter box I had for my old TV. These thoughts flashed through my head when I was silenced by Mr. Mayor's next words.

"I can close my eyes and surf hundreds of channels, which show the good and the bad of your world. Unfortunately, some of us, like humans, struggle to take the right path. A few of our young hares see the criminals prosper, choose this direction and try to take advantage of the rest of us. So our society has evolved much like yours. Our values are now often based on the media streaming through our heads."

The Mayor glanced upward, shook off a yawn, stretched his right front paw skyward, pointed up, and said, "Look up there at that darkling sky! (Darkling's a word I learned from you Abby, by the way.) It's the Northern Cross, the backbone of the Milky Way. Years ago these stars were just lights in the sky; they meant nothing. Now we see planets and constellations, thanks to the frequency."

"Do all of the residents of your city hear the frequency? And are all the jackrabbits giants?" I asked.

"A lot depends on the age of young hares. Some hear the audio and video stream as early as six months, and others take as long as a year to make sense of it all. Older rabbits tuned in quickly after the change. Many drink the water of our special artesian well and grow large within days, while others grow much slower. We haven't figured it all out yet. And for some reason, outsiders who come here also tune in, and their transformations often happen quickly as far as the frequency changes go. One important lesson we've learned is—wisdom comes with age and no matter how big you grow, you are only as large as the good you can bring to the rest of your fellow jacks."

He flopped his ears forward and yawned again. "Enough for now, you'd better start back to your camp. Following the paths out of here in the dark can be a bit tricky. How about we meet tomorrow at 2 P.M. and see how quick those dogs of yours are? We have a couple young hares who would love to put them through our obstacle course. We love to gamble on our young hares when they go up against a stray dog who wanders into our city. These hares are still small and make the chase very exciting."

"We'll see you tomorrow," Abby said, "and thanks, Mr. Mayor, for your insights."

We all waved goodbye and walked away, still in disbelief of the magical land that existed right smack dab in the middle of the beautiful Bruneau Sand Dune of Idaho. We crossed the dunes quickly back to the campground.

Eggy and Nasty, refreshed from their nap in the grass, loped swiftly and quietly through the sand. Nasty occasionally bit playfully at Eggy's long legs in a mischievous attempt to slow down the graceful Eggy.

"Eggy" is just a nickname for Eggnacio, a four year old black lab, who's the Michael Jordan of the long jump, fetching Frisbees, and a Michael Phelps in any kind of water. Nasty is just plain nasty, a one-year-old yellow lab with a pinkish, piggy-nose who loves to beat up on Eggy. He constantly trips him up on any trail they run together. If Eggy is the athlete, Nasty acts like Bart Simpson, always looking for the easiest way to get treats and attention, picking on his sibling, and never missing a chance to play a prank on his rival.

The dogs don't know it yet, but they will be put to the test tomorrow, entered into the big chase and race against a couple of alleged fast hares. I've seen my dogs in action plenty of times. I can't wait to see them race.

The campground was dark when we finally got back, but the glow of a yellow moon spilled out over the eastern slopes. The dunes gave off an eerie shine. The desert has its transitional moments: day slips into dusk, dusk fades into night and then the beautiful sun rises.

A long day in the hot desert sun had taken its toll. Our faces were red from the sun's rays, but luckily the sunscreen worked or all three of us would have been burnt like toast. The three of us drank large gulps of water from plastic bottles and the dogs buried their heads deep into the stainless steel bowls. Soon their dog tags clanked against the metal bowls, needing refills.

"What a day. Wow." Abby sighed and yawned, but said loud enough for Zach and me to hear.

"It's one I will certainly never forget," I said, my voice failing.

"We just got to keep this whole day to ourselves," Abby declared. "If it leaks out about N.J.R.C., every tourist in the U.S. will want a look at the giant rabbits and Mr. Mayor."

"You're right Abby. The desert here will be overrun with reporters and satellite trucks exploiting the hare's images all over the world," I agreed.

"Yeah, and this warning includes Jeffrey, Zach. I know he's your best friend, but if I see anything about this on Facebook, it will be the last post you write! This is our secret and no one else is to know. You got it?" Abby pointed her right index finger at Zach, and almost touched his nose. "Let's put our hands together and make a pact: Tell no one." Abby spoke in a whisper as if to hide the biggest secret in the world.

I played along with her childhood ritual. The three of us placed our hands in a circle and together we chanted, in chorus style: "Secret, secret, secret!"

After this display of solidarity, Abby asked, "Hey, Uncle Mike, can we get up early and go into Mountain Home and pick up some stuff, you know, supplies? We need ice, don't we? And maybe you could treat us to a hamburger at the Wendy's in town, please?" she asked in her most persuasive, innocent young eight-year-old voice. "I think Wendy's opens at ten."

The thought of a tasty hamburger, French fries and Internet access flashed through my mind, and Zach's, too, I'm sure. We looked at each other and knew: both of us wanted to be WIRED again to the net. This isolation from the digital world can be endured only so long. I thought, just for a second, how lucky the jacks were. Their ears work like wireless routers sifting through various frequencies all the time. I could get used to that, I thought to myself.

I promised a trip into town tomorrow; then we all dove into our separate tents. It had cooled down, so with the sleeping bags pulled up around our heads to keep out the desert night, I started dreaming about the big race—six-foot rabbits, sagebrush shady spots, a cool chase between dogs and rabbits, juicy hamburgers, and all of the magical excitement to come, when Eggy and Nasty crowded into my tent. Within minutes they were asleep, twitching about as their muscular legs snapped to the challenge of an imaginary chase. Usually Eggy snored like a newborn, but not tonight. How did he know he had a race to run tomorrow? Maybe it was some old memory of another adventurous chase. Just before I nodded off, Zach quietly entered my tent and said he had to tell me something.

"What's up, Zach? I'm listening."

He sat down beside me and started chewing on his fingernails. "Well, I keep thinking about Abby's warning to keep everything a secret. It's too late for that now. She's gonna kill me if she finds out! I already sent an email to my friend Jeffrey a couple months ago when Abby told me about the six-feet-tall jackrabbits we'd be seeing on our trip. I figured he's not gonna believe anything like that anyway. *I* didn't even believe it! But now I'm kind of worried, 'cause I even sent a map in my email to Jeffrey. He must have thought I was just kidding, right, Uncle Mike? I didn't tell *after* I made the promise." It was obvious that the whole situation was making him very uncomfortable.

"Well, just keep your promise now. That's all you can do. Something tells me N.J.R.C. and talking, tall rabbits aren't going to stay a secret for very long anyway. I'm sure others will find out about it sooner or later. Don't worry about it, Zach. Go get some sleep."

"Okay. Thanks. See you in the morning. I just know the dogs will win. I just know it."

"Well we'll see, won't we? Good night, Zach. Sweet dreams."

"Good night. Thanks."

Chapter Eleven:
Wiley and Casey's Cow Encounter

"Let's try that one," said Wiley Whiskers, the ornery rabbit who always hung around the switchyard trying to scam anybody he could. His sidekick brother, Casey, of course, was right by his side as he pointed to one of the black cows closest to the fence. "Let's try old Betsy there. That's what they call cows, isn't it?"

"I don't know what their names are, Wiley. I don't think they name every darn one of their cattle here," Casey answered back as he chewed on a piece of straw.

"Just give it here, that magic potion that we paid good money for. It's gonna make us rich as kings, little brother."

Wiley took the small sample of water they had on hand, safely tucked away in an eight-ounce plastic Pepsi bottle, and poured a couple ounces into the green water bowl Casey had stolen from old lady Thompson's cat. Then he climbed up on the fencing and held it up to the cow, which seemed perfectly willing to stand still and watch the two rabbits as they offered up something to drink in the hot Idaho weather. At first the cow just turned her head, but then it swung back around, and she took a couple sips. That was it. She didn't seem to be very thirsty. They offered the water a few more times, but the cow just turned away.

Casey looked at Wiley and asked, "Now what do we do?"

"We wait, what else dumb-cakes? We wait."

Both rabbits shrugged their shoulders and plunked to a sitting position on the ground. A mild breeze swept across their faces. Minutes ticked by while Wiley and Casey sat and stared at the cow, awaiting a miraculous change of stature.

Finally, Wiley couldn't take it anymore. "C'mon, get big, cow," he commanded, but in a normal sounding voice. "C'mon, what are ya waitin' for?"

"Yeah, c'mon, Betsy, start stretchin' those legs of yours to the sky," Casey chimed in. "You know how much extra meat we're gonna sell when you and all these here cows get giant-size?"

They glanced at each other, chewed away at their straw, and waited some more. Casey started tapping his right foot. Wiley wiggled from left to right, then right to left as he impatiently stared at the cow.

"Oh for Peter Rabbit's sake, I'm gonna make this here cow drink some more of the magic potion. I'm just wonderin' how much it takes." Wiley stood up and looked at Casey with a mischievous look on his face. Then Casey couldn't believe what happened next. Wiley tipped the plastic bottle to his own mouth and took two big swigs of the clear liquid. He moved his tongue around in circles and smacked his lips. "Hmm. Tasty. Let's see who sprouts up to giant-size first, me or little 'ol Betsy here."

"Wiley, you old daredevil! I thought we agreed, this here water was for the cows, so we could make our bundle of dough." The scheming partner crossed his arms and frowned.

"Just testin' the waters, old buddy, just testin' the magic waters." He laughed like a hyena while Casey kept right on frowning. "Now look, little buddy, if I grow up right now and start a towerin' over ya, just remember I ain't prejudiced or anything against nobody just 'cause of color, politics or size, okay?" He grinned from rabbit-ear-to-rabbit-ear. "Now c'mon, Betsy dear, drink some more. You're our scientific experiment." He held the kitty bowl in front of the cow. This time the cow took a few more sips. "See, Casey, I got me a way with the girls."

"You might just have a way with the girls but you can't even charm the bell off this here cow. Give old Casey that bottle. I'll show you how to get that water down this stubborn cow's throat." Casey used his big rabbit feet to jump up onto the fence post, then leapt right on the back of the old cow. He held on to one of its ears, the one with the name tag hanging down, and stuck the bottleneck right between the lower and upper lips of the now restless two-thousand-pound critter.

The eyes of the once tranquil animal began to change from enjoying a quiet afternoon in the pasture to a small fire burning in each pupil. Flames began to build and before you knew it, the beast had had it! Her giant nostrils opened up like a fireman's hose, water shot out, and it was then that the scrawny Casey knew he had most likely made a very bad decision. With one snort and violent headshake, the cow threw Casey five feet in the air, over the fence and right down on Idaho's famous prickly cactus.

The laughs from Wiley almost drowned out the screams bellowing from Casey's distorted mouth. He screamed, bad-mouthing the cow, and got busy yanking at the cactus needles sticking to him all over as if he were some cursed rabbit voodoo doll. Wiley couldn't help it, he turned his head, but every few seconds let out another snicker.

They finally settled down, and the two dreamy rabbits began their impatient waiting once more. Wiley kept looking at his hands and feet and feeling his head and ears to see if he was growing bigger. Then he couldn't resist, and chewed out the cow: "C'mon, cow, get big! Get BIG! What the heck are ya waitin' for?"

"Yeah, cow, c'mon, we ain't got all day. We're business hares here. We gotta get this show on the road!"

"We ain't no circus show, Casey. Who talks like that? And it ain't a show, it's an enterprise. Wise up, rabbit, wise up." Wiley stared even harder, right into the cow's eyes, then turned back to Casey. "Hey, when I start breakin' out of my clothes here," – Wiley liked to dress up like a cowboy sometimes – "you make sure you get me some big size human clothes, okay? I'm countin' on ya for that favor, okay?"

"Sure thing. No problem. The Wilkersons got a clothesline. They're always hanging stuff out to dry."

"Hey, look at my right hand. You think it's getting a little bigger? Looks to me like it's swellin' up." Wiley held out his right paw, turning it up and down for Casey to inspect.

"I don't know, Wiley, looks the same to me. The cow, too. Don't appear nothin's growin' big, not you and not Betsy here. Not yet, anyway," Casey sighed.

"Shucks! I got it, I know what the problem is. We need more water. Let's go talk to the boss again and see if he got that tanker truck we talked about. We'll drain that well dry and sip water 'till the whole herd of cows, and you and me, are all big success experiments. Whaddaya say, partner?" He jumped up to a standing position and took one final look at his hands, which were the same exact size as always.

"Okay, partner. I'm right behind ya." Casey laid the bowl down on the ground in front of the cow and the two of the scheming rabbits hopped off. "See ya later there, Betsy!" Casey yelled back at the cow.

"C'mon, Casey, we got us some important business to take care of. I just know it's gonna work when we get our hands on a whole lot more of that magic water. C'mon. Let's hightail it back to the boss, get that tanker rollin'. I know just where he might be." Wiley led the way.

"Okay, Wiley, right behind ya."

Holding on hard to their get big/get rich schemes as they hopped along with a golden sunshine warming their fur, they headed over to Maxie's Country Store, where Wiley figured Bossy would be flirting with the gal he loved, the one who wanted nothing to do with him.

Chapter Twelve: Time to Warn the Mayor

Morning breaks early in the desert. Dancing waves of red light fade across the horizon as the sun slowly rises. With the sky clear as a mountain stream, the day started fast and furious. Abby was up before the sun crested the big dune, and woke Zach and me. Eggy and Nasty were already pulling at their leashes waiting for the first romp over the cool sand. I made it a short run, to conserve their winning edge. Still, they were breathing hard after their exercise.

We stopped first at Maxie's, a little country store, by the freight yard so I could get some coffee. Maxie, a middle-aged lady with grey hair worn up in a bun and two missing teeth, was friendly enough. We just happened to show up the same time as old Bossy Kincaid, a well-known cattle herder in the area, wearing dirty overalls and a John Deer hat. I couldn't believe my ears. Neither could Abby and Zach.

"Yeah, Maxie, I hired me a driver and his buddy. Their gonna head out to that desert tomorrow with a big tanker truck and haul all that magic water back from N.J.R.C."

Abby and Zach looked up at me with their eyebrows raised to alert level and eyes open as wide as could be.

"My cows are gonna be giants! I'll get richer than ever and then I can make you my little missus. What do you say to that, sweetheart?"

"Oh, I think you're delusional, as usual, if you think I'm ever marrying the likes of you, Bossy Kincaid." She dusted some shelves off and tried to ignore him. Bossy moved in to hug her, but Maxie quickly backed away. She couldn't stand the smell of alcohol and bad breath spilling out his mouth. "Besides, you're supposed to be takin' it easy with that bad heart a yours, ain't that what the Doc said?"

"Oh I ain't worried about my ticker. I'm strong as a horse. The boys will be out at the old slaughterhouse at five, and we're gonna start workin' our own magic on gettin' us that there fancy water."

I wondered if I'd have to intervene if the drunken old guy got out of hand. Meanwhile, we shopped around the store, picking up whatever items we needed for our next night out.

"C'mon, Maxie, sweetie, you know you're the only one for me. I just gotta make ya my bride. Now please, honey, come to your senses," he begged.

Ignoring his marriage offer, Maxie got back to the subject of his scheme to get rich. "Now why you wanna go ahead and send a truck in there, scare them rabbits and mess up that beautiful land? What you wanna do that for?"

"Just 'cause I can, sweet pea. Just 'cause I can. And I already told ya, you heard the stories, I get them cows all doubled or tripled in size, look at the profits!" he shouted, then hiccupped four times in a row.

"And who says it works on cows? You're so greedy you can't even think straight. Now go on, get on home to your ranch and kill some more innocent cows. I told ya a million times, I'm a vegetarian and I don't want nothin' to do with the likes of you and your business. Now go on out of here, Bossy, or I'll be calling my brother." She whisked her duster at him.

I walked up to the cash register now, hoping the guy would leave peacefully.

"Hello there," Maxie said, "don't mind him, he was just leavin'. Anything else I can get you?" Bossy frowned at us, blew a kiss to Maxie, turned and stomped out.

"Well, we need some ice. I don't see any bags in the thing outside."

"Like I say, don't mind him. He's just the town drunk. Oh sorry, we're all out of ice. Should have some in by tomorrow. You can pick some up at the local supermarket though, Albertsons, over by Mountain Home." Maxie asked Zach and Abby, "So, you kids are camping out there at Bruneau Sand Dune?"

"Yeah, we're having fun," Abby said. "Today our dogs are gonna race some rabbits! I know they'll win." She held up a Hershey's candy bar and gave me a pleading eye.

I shook my head no and pointed to the fruit and nuts on the counter that we'd be buying instead.

Maxie stared into the kid's eyes. "What rabbits your dogs racing? You ain't heard no talking rabbits now, have you, or seen that big Mayor character everybody's always talking about but never sees, have ya?"

Just then a few other customers walked in the door.

"Well, sorry, ma'am," I said, "we're in a hurry. We have to go. C'mon, kids, dogs are waiting for us outside." I rushed them toward the door.

"Well, wait a minute...you didn't answer..." Maxie tried to get an answer, but the kids and I hurried out of there before they had to either lie or confess that, indeed, we knew all about the new inhabitants of New Jack Rabbit City and were headed right back there after we got our breakfast and ice.

"Uncle Mike, it's a good thing we have the race today, so we know we can talk to the Mayor," Abby said as we climbed into our truck.

"Yeah," Zach agreed, "any stupid trucks will tear up all their land and probably run right over any small rabbits living here."

"Now, kids, listen," I instructed, wanting to be clear before we hit the road, "we're going to try and warn the Mayor, but I want you to stick close while all of this is going on, okay?"

"Okay," Abby and Zach promised simultaneously. "It's probably a good thing we ran into that Bossy guy, huh?" Abby added.

"Yes. I think the Mayor needs to be warned. Not sure what he can do. But we'll tell him today what we overheard.

"Uncle Mike," Zach asked, "why did that guy act so crazy?"

"Well, Zach, for one thing, he's in love. And he drinks too much. You stay away from that guy, both of you."

"He scares me, and I don't want him bothering the Mayor or the other rabbits," Abby said.

"Me neither," Zach added.

"Well, we'll see what we can do. Just stay away from him and any trucks you might see in the area, okay, promise?" I waited for their promise.

"We promise." Abby and Zach both crossed their hearts.

"Okay, let's get that tasty breakfast, ice, and get Eggy and Nasty ready for the race. It's a big day for them."

"Yeah, they're so fast, I bet they can beat any rabbit on the planet," Abby boasted.

"Well, we'll see. Won't we? We'll see. Sure they'll do their best, that's for sure. But first let's go to Mountain Home. I need more coffee and I know you guys are all psyched up about eating at Wendy's." The kids couldn't wait to eat out and then return to what they considered to be a magical kingdom—a place where rabbits talked and grew big like humans.

"Hey, Casey," Wiley said, as the family with the dogs got in their truck, "check this out. I'm thinkin', maybe they're headed out to see the giant jacks? Probably camping and just in town for some supplies. Whaddaya say we follow them? We just gotta make King Kongs outta Bossy's cattle, just like we talked about. He says he'll cut us in for a good amount as long as we can tell him where the artesian well is for sure. I bet that kid's got a map in his backpack or in that Chevy truck of theirs. I just bettcha."

Casey nodded. "Hey, there's Bossy's pickup, we can hitch a ride with him, tell him to follow them. Let's see if Bossy ordered the tanker truck yet!"

After hopping in the pickup, Wiley kept glancing at his front paws to see if they'd gotten any bigger at all after his swigs of water. Nothing yet. Finally Wiley's hare brain kicked in and he realized he had probably wasted his good money. That old rabbit, Bruno, who hangs around at the switchyard, he never should have paid him. That water the cow and he were sipping on must have been just plain old water, no magic, no nothing.

Bossy informed the other two schemers that he was going to get him some breakfast in Mountain Home, anyway, so he agreed to follow the other family since that's where they were headed. Then he'd head over to Albertsons to see if the big truck had gotten into town yet. The old drunk still couldn't believe he was talking to rabbits. When it all first happened, their first conversation, he almost gave up the bottle. But that only lasted a day.

It was an exception, the fact that the two daring rabbits decided to show a human they could talk. It didn't happen often because they figured somebody would scoop them up and sell them to a circus. But Wiley saw dollar signs with the giant cow scheme and trusted, of all people, a big-mouthed drinker.

With news of the truck coming to town, Wiley's heart began to race. He couldn't wait to get his paws on that real magic water! And they weren't far behind the man and his kids. Wiley started plotting, telling Casey and Bossy that whenever they parked, it would be a great time to try and hop in the family's truck and see if they had a map of N.J.R.C. inside.

"Yeah, Bossy, when they go in somewhere, Casey and me, we'll get that map finally for ya, so you'll know where to send the tanker."

"You rotten rabbits, I thought you had the map already. You sneakin' couple of liars. You was gonna let me hire my drivers and bring the tanker in without ever even knowin' where we was supposed to go. Why, I oughta..." He picked up his whiskey bottle and held it over Wiley's head for a few seconds then took a swig and turned back to watch the road.

"We're on it, Boss," Wiley said. "You just get us in the same parking lot as that family there and we'll get us that map, for sure."

Casey stared into Wiley's eyes and wondered, What if the map's not in their truck? What if they lock it? But he didn't say a word.

After a good stretch on the long flat road, the Snake River flowed steadily to the west beneath us, slowing at a wide passage as our truck raced across the long bridge toward our destination. Mountain Home, population fifteen-thousand, used to be called Rattle Snake Junction, and served as a stop on the Overland Stage Line. The town's name is deceptive, though. Mountain Home could well be called Oceanside or Seaside, since it's not in the mountains but at the base, sitting flat as a pancake in a sea of sagebrush and tumbleweeds.

I asked Zach to turn the CD player down; the kids love their loud music. As we rode along, it was evident that this was cattle country; huge feedlots blanketed the hillside, many of them old Kincaid's, no doubt. Hundreds of cows dotted the landscape, looking like white and black checkerboard squares. Ironically, for many of the cows in the area, after the fattening lots, their last stop would be at the Wendy's where we were just now entering.

"Hamburgers and fries, breakfast of champions, right, Uncle Mike?" Abby teased.

"It's an exception, Abby and Zach, an exception, and don't you forget it! Tomorrow it's back to Cheerios and bananas," I said seriously but with a smile on my face.

"Where you gonna eat, Boss, the family's parked there at Wendy's," Wiley asked.

"Yeah, we don't want to be too conspicious, right partners?"

"Right, Boss, you mean *conspicuous*?" Wiley corrected him.

"Whatever, you think rabbits are smarter than humans? Ain't never gonna happen. I'm eatin' at Grinde's Diner. You guys stay put."

Sure enough, when the family went to eat, Zach forgot to lock the door. It was as easy as stealing carrots from a farmer's garden. There it was, sitting right under a newspaper on the dashboard, scribbled on school notebook paper, a map of N.J.R.C. spelling it out in bold letters. Wiley snuck in, grabbed it and hopped back to Bossy's truck.

"I got it Casey! Look, right here in big letters, drawings to everything, the way in from the dune, the beach, and there it is! Looks like they call it a 'springhouse.' And it's circled; right here, the artesian well. Wonder if there's more than one. I don't see no others, do you, Casey?" He handed over the amateurishly drawn map.

When Bossy returned, he took another swig of whiskey and laughed out loud. "Well, well, looks like the bunny brains came through, what do ya know. Guess we'll be heading over to Albertsons now, hitch up with my drivers. Good job, boys, good job." He slobbered a little and coughed several times.

Wiley and Casey sat back, grinning, and just knew they'd be growing to six-feet-tall within days, and with Bossy's cattle they'd get rich for sure.

For the kids and me, it seemed like breakfast lasted no time and soon we were driving on the outskirts of town to Albertsons for ice and any other necessary supplies. A large cattle yard stretched a half mile long to the west of the food store, and a large tandem water truck idled in the morning sun of the Albertsons' parking lot, next to a nearby feedlot. A pair of drivers, cowboys, stood in front of the truck, kicking the ground, spitting out some chew, and seemingly waiting for orders.

"Oh, oh, look, that's some big rig, I bet it can hold thousands of gallons of water," I speculated. "Got to be the one that Kincaid talked about." We all looked at each other with concern in our eyes.

Inside the store we grabbed a few necessities and ice. The checkout cashier, a familiar face, seemed a bit different today with an inquisitive look on her face, as if she was looking for some answers.

"I hear you've been camped at Bruneau for the last few days," she said, not looking up at any one of us as she passed our items through the price scanner.

A bit shocked, our eyes all met at once as Zach answered, "Yeah, camped at the park since Friday."

"I hear some kinda rumor about big jackrabbits in the park, some talk of magic water flowing right outta the ground, you guys seen any of that silliness?" This time she looked up, right at the kids.

"We're just flying kites and running our dogs in the sand," Abby replied quickly. "The only wildlife we've seen is a couple of lizards and a small cottontail the dogs kicked up."

"So you guys know nothing at all about any of this, hmm?" she persisted.

This brought a sharp response from Abby. "Why should we?"

"I hear things at the store, suppose you never met that big jack dressed like a clown, have ya?"

"Ma'am, we're just camping out and having a good time, got no idea what you're talkin' about," Zach stepped up to the plate. "You got us confused, ma'am, we're just camping out, and that's it!" We grabbed all of our stuff, made a beeline for the doors and stepped out into the rising heat of the day, not saying a word. Now we knew for sure. New Jack Rabbit City was no secret anymore, and we just had to warn the Mayor. As we hustled out, we passed the two trucker cowboys coming into the store, so we listened in as the two characters spoke to each other, as if we were tuned-in rabbits with our ears stretched high.

"I'm gonna bring my rifle, maybe my double-barrel shotgun, just in case any of them rabbits has a mind to start a war over that magic water," the dark tanned driver told his partner.

"This pump we got should suck that spring dry in no time flat," the shorter one replied. "But we'll bring in more trucks if we have to."

His words echoed in my head, and I shuddered at the words, "Suck that spring dry. We'll bring in more trucks if we have to." Abby was quite startled. I knew she'd heard it, too.

"We gotta get back to camp and straight back to N.J.R.C. and warn the Mayor!" she shouted as we hustled the food and ice into the truck.

Then Eggy and Nasty, hair on their backs standing at attention, both gave a sudden jerk at their leashes. Eggy broke free, the leash ripped from my hand.

Within seconds he was at the feet of two jackrabbits by another pickup truck, and they all kicked up dust from the parched dirt as the rabbit dashed away, one under the wheels of the tanker truck, the other right under the fence into the cattle yard.

Eggy braked hard at the fence, ignoring my cries to come back, while the big jack sped under the feet of nearly two hundred head of cattle. Hooves danced around him, kicked and sent him flying a couple of times, once high enough to go head long into the rump of an old cow. With the ping-pong action, the rabbit lasted thirty seconds before he made it to the fence and went airborne from one final kick into an empty field next to the pen.

I got Eggy back under control and we all laughed at the escapade. Laughter vanished, though, as concern stirred up in our voices once again.

"You're right, kids, let's get going. The dogs have a race to run and we need to warn the Mayor." After petting Eggy and Nasty on the heads, I whispered in their ears, "Nice job on that frisky rabbit. Now get some rest before your big chase." Then I put the truck in gear and left the store, leaving a cloud of dust.

"Oh man, what a wallop. Oh my aching head, and back, and butt. I'm gonna get them dogs for this. If it ain't cows, it's dogs always messin' with us. I feel like my ribs are cracked. Am I bleedin'?" Casey whined, tears in his eyes now. "Just tell me, Wiley, how bad is it?"

"Oh, it's serious all right. I see a couple skinned areas. Let's get you to a hospital," Wiley laughed. "I'm just jokin' with ya. I just see a couple little scraped areas on ya, that's all."

"Go ahead, joke. Maybe I'll have to lie here, never walk again."

"Well, you'll never know unless you try. Here, let me help you up. Can you stand up?" Wiley got a good hold under his arms and boosted him up.

"Oh man. I'm gonna get me some of that magic water, get super big, and work on my paybacks, that's for sure." Casey hopped a few steps and rubbed his head.

"All right, all right. So you think you're gonna live then?"

"I guess. Oh my butt hurts! Darn them dogs and cows!" He hopped a little faster and both rabbits headed back over toward Bossy Kincaid's truck.

Chapter Thirteen: New Places, New Faces

Idaho, Bruneau Sand Dune, the desert, New Jack Rabbit City, it was all so different from Chicago city life, the hustle and bustle. But all the hares, even the South-Siders, who'd camped on the outskirts in private with Mrs. Palmer, were breathing it all in and liking it. In fact, by morning, Caponey gave the orders to make camp closer to town and as soon as he heard it was true about the magic water, he was loving it in N.J.R.C.

The Mayor and the rest of the inhabitant hares knew they had their hands full, though. In fact, an important advisory council meeting took place to draw up an action plan. Most of the families and newcomers, nobody had a problem with but, Caponey, that was another story. Mr. Mayor had one quick talk with all of the "gang" members and knew the only real problem was the Caponey character. As soon as he got the ego-ridden true gangster wannabe under control, all his followers would blend into N.J.R.C. like a backdrop painting of those dogs sitting around a table playing poker and having a good old time.

Of course, the Mayor always saw the good in rabbits; sometimes that was the problem. Some council members thought their fearless, faithful leader was waiting far too long to set straight the few corrupted, criminal thinking rabbits living there already. But Mr. Mayor assured them all, moral transformation took time. The changes all had to come from within and on the troubled rabbit's own timeline. Besides, if anything got too out of hand, he had his magical waters and ways to take care of anything that came up. So he always told the council members and the rest of the inhabitants, "Keep working our natural magic on them, that potent potion called love. They'll all come around and no worries. No worries."

In the meantime, Rush and Ryker were hopping around the desert looking for their mother, wondering if she had made it there yet, and felt like a couple of Lewis and Clark explorers, discovering their own new America. Mostly, though, they couldn't wait to see their mom again and find out what she thought about New Jack Rabbit City.

Of course Rush's heart was still broken because Wrigley didn't hop on the train right alongside of her when she needed him and had already told him how she thought he could be the one for her, if he'd only change his ways. Now she just didn't know. Her heart hurt, but her mind ached worse, since now she didn't think she could depend on him when she needed him most. Love meant a person was willing to give his/her life to save a loved one. All she had asked him to do was get on a train.

She wrote the following entry in her journal: "If love between two is not the most sacred, most powerful thing in the world, a spiritual connection when two become one, and protection of that love and soul mate's existence is not vital to being, then, forget it. Love is NOT the answer, not with that hare, anyway."

Rush knew she'd survive. The thing is, she was just beginning to feel hope again in her heart and truly live again. Her dad always told her: "Life goes on sweetie; life goes on. Please let it go on with love in your heart. There is no better way to live." Those were words she heard from her dear father just weeks before he died.

"Rush, Rush, look, there's a couple of the tall rabbits, right there, over there by that tree," Ryker whispered and pointed.

Rush forgot her worries and conflicts, looked up and sure enough, there they were, a couple of giant hares. She'd seen a few from the distance, but these were fairly close. There they were, talking up a storm, just as if they were humans.

"C'mon Ryker, let's go the other way. We don't want to bother them. Let's go swimming. What do ya say, little brother?" She knew he'd be thrilled.

"Yeah Sis, let's head for that beach. Auntie Annie is making a good lunch for us, too. She told me this morning. This is the life: swimming, hiking, big rabbits, miracles and all. You think you wanna be six-feet-tall? I do. Man, I could really give someone the karate chops then." He waved his hands in the air and performed a couple kicks.

"I don't know. Maybe four feet? Six feet is kind of tall. And I cannot picture my little brother six-feet-tall and towering over me. You've got to weigh the pros and cons to things, you know. Just like Dad used to tell us, 'Always weigh the pros and cons.'" She'd taken on the job of mentor, and it felt good, like she was all grown up. She added, "Besides, we've seen a lot of normal-sized hares, too, just like us, and they seem to be perfectly content. The Mayor says it's our choice, if and when the time is right."

After a refreshing swim at the beach, they hopped back to their campsite, which was host now to many Chicago hares. Everybody was getting all settled in. Bobbiteer and Ryker were buddies now, planning on fishing sometime and watching the big chase race together. Dogs against rabbits, racing and jumping over obstacle stuff, they couldn't wait to see that! But Bobbiteer insisted to his parents that he still hated the transition and just wanted to go home.

The Wyndhameers knew it would take some more time and adjusting for Bobbiteer, but they were so happy and knew the move was right for them all, especially Bobbiteer. The Arlingtons, too. They felt as if N.J.R.C. was the perfect place to retire. Until, that is, they met the South-Siders and wondered why some bad karma from Chicago had to follow them all the way out to Idaho, their new paradise, and maybe spoil it all.

Putz, he got busy finding anything he could in the sand. Came across a couple quarters, then spotted a turquoise ring, a pair of flip-flops, and even an old fishing pole. Took all of it back to his site, of course. Said he was going to build a storage shed and start him a flea market business.

Caponey, all he wanted to do was have another heart-to-heart talk with the big rabbit, Mr. Mayor, get his hands on that magic water, and relax all day sipping and dreaming big.

Wrigley spent his time catering to Mrs. Palmer and went on a search for Rush and Ryker, promised he'd find her two kids and bring them right to her. She begged him to hurry. She still had to give her leg time to heal, so she decided to leave it up to Wrigley. Mrs. Palmer hated to admit it, but he was kind of growing on her. A lot of potential, she thought to herself, a lot of potential. But she was still going to keep her eye on him.

When Wrigley had trouble finding Rush and Ryker's campsite, he asked for help from the Mayor, and he got it. He thanked Mr. Mayor and off he went. He had hopped off in three different directions, but sure enough it was the fourth one that would lead him to the kids. Wrigley knew the kids couldn't wait to see their mom, just as Mrs. Palmer sat waiting and was aching to see them and know they were safe. (I'll share more about that reunion later.)

Meigs, Bronzey, Fuzzy and Mugsey, they were the ones working the hardest toward their new dreams. They planned to spend day and night writing songs. The Mayor told them he had connections, thought they had great talent, encouraged them to keep it up, their Rappin' Rabbits singing foursome. So that's just what they did. Caponey and Dice made a promise to step up to the plate as their managers—when the time is right.

RAPPIN' RABBITS (A Change of Hearts)

Talkin' rabbits yeah yeah, singin' rabbits yeah.
Talkin' rabbits yeah yeah, singin' rabbits yeah.

We're The Rappin' Rabbits and we got us a new life ya see.
Moved out here from Chicago, gonna see what life can be.
Gonna see what life can be, got us a new life ya see.
Gonna see what life can be, got us a new life ya see.

Once upon a time, we were into crime.
Hustled for the dime, in the alleyways and grime.
Our boss, Caponey, yeah, he even did some time.
From the city lights of Chicago, to the sandy dunes of Idaho,
what a change, what a life now, what a way to go.

Chicago hares moved west, ya see.
Jack Rabbit City's the place to be.
Left the South side, wild side,
the Loop and Lake Shore Drive.
Miss the lake, that shine, that one and only skyline.
But Idaho's workin' for us.
It's all turnin' out just fine.

Talkin' rabbits yeah yeah, singin' rabbits yeah.
Talkin' rabbits yeah yeah, singin' rabbits yeah.

New faces, new places, changin' our gangster ways.
From city lights to sandy dunes, starry nights and sunny days.
Singing gigs, dreamin' big. Say Alvin, all the rest of you—
we're not chipmunks, but our funk will rule!
Soon our songs will be sellin' too.

We got sandy hills to climb, all that sunshine.
A big rabbit gave us a line, how to give up our life of crime.
We can sing, we can dream big.
We can talk and grow six-feet-tall.

After all, after all,
there's magic in the water here,
magic for us all.
New Jack Rabbit City's the place to be.
We even tuned in to the frequency!

Talkin' rabbits yeah yeah, singin' rabbits yeah.
Talkin' rabbits yeah yeah, singin' rabbits yeah.

Dreams are for chasin', you gotta quit wastin'.
Start tryin', stop cryin' and dyin'.
Can't let life pass you by.
You gotta start tryin', stop cryin' and dyin'.
Can't let life pass you by.
Just try, just try, just try.

Get up, get up, get tough, get tough.
Get up, get up, get tough, get tough.
You gotta start tryin', stop cryin' and dyin'.
Can't let life pass you by.
Just try, just try, just try, just try.

We're The Rappin' Rabbits, we got us a new life ya see.
Moved out here from Chicago, gonna see what life can be.
Gonna see what life can be, got us a new life ya see.
Gonna see what life can be.

Talkin' rabbits yeah yeah, singin' rabbits yeah.
Talkin' rabbits yeah yeah, singin' rabbits yeah.
Talkin' rabbits yeah yeah, singin' rabbits yeah.
Talkin' rabbits. Talkin' rabbits. Talkin' rabbits.
Yeah.

PUTZ (I'm Livin' the Good Life Now)

Say God, hey, this is Putz here on Earth. Hi.
Are you up there somewhere
in that Idaho clear blue sky?
Yeah, this is Putz. I never asked for much.
But you came through for me anyway.
What can I say?
Again, this is Putz.
 I'm thinkin' I should thank you.
Thank you. Thank you, very, very much.

'Cause I'm livin' the good life now.
No more hardscrabble day to day.
Found a better way, found a better way.
I'm livin' the good life now.
No more hardscrabble day to day.
Found a better way. Found a better way.
All the cool things I find at the beach every day!
Found a better way, found a better way.

Got change to hang onto.
Got work I love to do.
Just 'cause you came through.
Just 'cause you came through.

All us Chicago Hares, we got us a new life ya see.
All 'cause we made the move here
to New Jack Rabbit City.
And like all those other good hares
always thankin' you,
well, this is Putz and I'm thankin' ya too.
I'm thankin' ya too.

'Cause I'm livin' the good life now.
No more hardscrabble day to day.
Found a better way. Found a better way.
I'm not much of a singer God,

so, so just bear with me,
but I have a song for you—so here it is.

I'm livin' the good life now.
No more hardscrabble day to day.
Found a better way, found a better way.
All the cool things I find at the beach every day.
Found a better way. Found a better way.

All us Chicago Hares, we got us a new life ya see.
All 'cause we made the move here
to New Jack Rabbit City.
And like all those other good hares
always thankin' you,
well this is Putz and I'm thankin' ya too.
I'm thankin' ya too.

'Cause I'm livin' the good life now.
No more hardscrabble day to day.
Found a better way, found a better way.
I'm livin' the good life now.
No more hardscrabble day to day.
Found a better way. Found a better way.

Oh yeah, I'm dancin' now God.
Got the sand here beneath my toes, my furry toes.
Can you see me dancin' God? I'm dancin'.
I'm dancin' now God,
right here on the sandy beach.

'Cause I'm livin' the good life.
Oh yeah this is Putz.
I never asked for much, but I had to thank you.
Thank you very, very much. Thank you God.
Thank you very, very much.
'Cause I'm livin' the good life now.
Thank you God, thank you God,
very, very much.

Chapter Fourteen: Uncertainties

As far as Caponey's kidnap scheme, the Mayor had heard enough. How ridiculous, using a sweet little hare like Brooklyn Palmer to try and weasel his way into New Jack Rabbit City and try and exchange her for magic water. Mr. Mayor and the entire advisory council did not take kindly to this type of extortion attempt. Oddly enough, though, the council did vote to give Caponey and the rest of the South-Siders (whom they really had no problem with) a chance, the benefit of the doubt. After all, the Mayor never stopped believing or professing to others that goodness can certainly prevail over evil.

The uncertain factor, however, was Caponey. The other Chicago hares, no problem. In fact, most of them were delightful new residents, even Caponey's followers. But the "leader," some leader Mr. Mayor thought, he was a piece of work. A true broken piece of work and there were no guarantees that what was broken could be fixed.

Here's what Mr. Mayor had to say to Caponey at a face-off during their one on one meeting: "Now, Mr. Caponey, as I've said and informed the others, we've decided to let you continue to reside here in N.J.R.C. Also, as far as your request for the magic water – drink up. In fact, drink all you want. Learn whatever you want and need to learn. Go where your heart and mind take you. But I assure you, for bad choices, there are bad consequences. Not only that, but we have so much goodness here in N.J.R.C., promise, and hope. We can use help on many projects, all positive, constructive pathways, if you so choose to participate."

The Mayor was just about fed up with the sighs coming from the gangster sitting across from him, but he continued his speech.

"The thing is *Mister* Caponey, I assure you if we decide you are not willing to change and contribute, we have our very simple, 'magical' ways of making sure that you disappear from here forever." The Mayor grinned and paused to see if Caponey wanted to say anything.

"Yeah, like what?" He crossed his arms and leaned back.

"Oh like I say, how would you like to shrink to the size of a mouse? You know, as you've discovered, this magic water is the real thing. If some water can make us grow bigger, don't you think the opposite just might be true, too?" Instantly Mr. Mayor stood up and towered over Caponey.

Caponey looked up into the Mayor's eyes. "Well I wanna be big! That's why I'm here. You know that. I just wanna get big; then I'll leave all yous behind, go back to Chicago and be able to knock those North-Siders on their butts. They ain't even brave enough to travel out here and see for themselves if this is all true or not."

"Okay, okay. So you wanna be big and strong."

"That's right, you got it. Ain't nobody gonna stop me neither!" Caponey stood up and tried to stretch his ears up so he could at least appear a little taller to match up with the giant standing before him.

"Fine. You drink that water. We'll see what happens. But in the meantime, Mrs. Palmer is free! Ya here? No more acting like some *America's Most Wanted* kidnappers. You got that?" he asked in his most commanding voice.

"Yeah, yeah. I got it. Long as I get my water, ain't no use for her any ways. I just needed a little insurance, that's all, wasn't gonna fluff her fur up or hurt her or anything." Caponey finished his sentence, started coughing and asked if he could have another glass of magic water.

"Sure. No problem. Here you go." Mr. Mayor grabbed a bottle from the cooler he had sitting next to him. He knew the meeting would go better if he had some of the miracle worker liquid on hand.

"Gee, thanks! I'm kinda gettin' to like you. I get to be your size, what you say we become pals? I could use someone like you," Caponey said excitedly, then gulped down the water. "You ever think about movin' to a real city? You'd like Lake Michigan and all the pretty lights of Chicago at night."

"We'll see, my friend, we'll see. Now for starters, about some of that positive work I was telling you about. I could use a few of you to help us with a big race we've got between a few of our young hares and a couple pretty healthy dogs. Should be a lot of fun. What do you say? Join in some good clean fun for a change."

"Yeah, sure. Why not? I'll get some of the boys to come. The girls can watch. Are we done here now?" Caponey took his last swig.

Caponey knew the big chase was the talk of the day. Nobody was going to miss that. The rest of the gang already said they wanted to help with the event: Rabbits vs. Dogs Chase. Being a bookie in the past, in the big city, Caponey did think a while about an angle to make him some dough. He surprised himself, though. His mind was all caught up in drinking as much water as he could. He kept focusing on getting bigger and bigger. But it wasn't out of the question, if he could make a little money on the side, that'd be just fine with him.

The Mayor kept trying to get all of the South-Siders to do constructive things. He was truly hoping for the best, a change of hearts, from hardened to soft, loving hares again. He'd done it before many times, the conversion, worked his magic on wayward hares or rabbits. He wasn't even sure the South-Siders wanted to stay in N.J.R.C., like Caponey with all his talk about going back to Chicago to rule the streets when he finished growing to giant-size. But if any of them did want to stick around, they'd have to change their ways. That the Mayor knew for sure.

Caponey handed his empty bottle to the Mayor. "Can I get one more refill?"

The Mayor obliged. "Oh, by the way, one more thing. The girls and those other two, I heard them singing last night. Outstanding! I think you got something there with your Rappin' Rabbits. You know I got a lot of connections. We could use some entertainment here at N.J.R.C. and around Idaho, maybe around the world. We've been kind of infiltrating with the humans, and they're starting to accept us more and more; the fact that we can talk and are as intelligent as them, I'd say more so. Something tells me you've got a hunger for money and a good sense for managing things. Maybe we could work something out there, too, you know on the *productive* side of things." He raised his eyebrows and gave Caponey a teacher-to-student look.

"What do you want me to do here, run some kinda *Hare's Got Talent* show or somethin'? I ain't no Brit. Maybe you're confusin' me with that Cowell dude." Caponey laughed and shook his head left and right.

"Maybe. What's wrong with that? Keep ya busy, out of trouble," the Mayor said, trying to talk his way into the heart of the hardened hare.

"Like you said, big fella, we'll see. We'll see. Let me go talk to *my* advisors, what do ya say to that?"

"Okay, okay, Mister Caponey. Get back to me as soon as possible. Enjoy your water and stay here. No doubt fate will run its course for N.J.R.C. and for you." The Mayor offered his right paw.

Caponey shook paws and was on his way back to the campsite. He really wanted to get back to his gang, where he was boss, not having some big giant rabbit trying to make him into some soft, mushy, boring good hare or something. All he knew was that the water was kicking in. He looked down at his toes and sure enough they were extending out an inch longer than before. He could swear he felt growing pains, too, as if his whole body was starting to stretch upward. When he got back to the gang, none of them could believe it. Two inches taller than Dice. Caponey was as happy as a kid at Christmas Eve who just got to open the best present ever.

Yes sir, Caponey had big plans, *BIG* plans. Big dreams, too, and they were starting to come true.

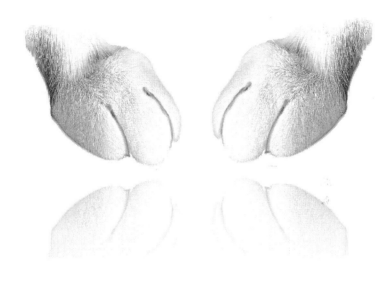

KING CAPONEY

(Yawn) Oh man I'm tired, oh, long day here in the desert.
Oh man, woo, oh, stretchin' my long furry legs, yeah.
Hey, my name is Caponey, but you ugh, you can call me King
or Boss or gang leader of the South-Siders,
the idea master of lots of things.

Yeah (yawn) oh man I'm tired today, oh long day, just thinkin'.
For instance, when I was just a kid,
Pop told me, "Cap, you'll never make it big."
Well I showed him, yes I did.
Got me a big time bookie job, bookie gig, yes I did,
yes I did, yes I did.

Oh, let me stretch out here a little bit.
Oh man, oh man, my legs are gettin' long, long, longer every day.
My arms are getting long. I'm gettin' tall man, I'm gettin' tall.
Let me take a drink of water here.

Ya see, Pop was kinda rough on me, but that was just his way.
Ma, well, she was just tired, so much so, she up and died one day.
Yep, then Pop gave up and that was it.
No brothers, no sisters, anybody, nobody but me.
Had to make do anyway I could, cause I was on my own,
ya see, ya see.

But I got lucky, got me a family, oh my buddy, Dice.
All the rest of them South-Siders, ya see,
they turned to me, ya see, ya see, they turned to me.
We all became one motley crew, one special family,
um hmm, um hmm.

We dreamed, we schemed, we dreamed, we schemed.
We dreamed, we schemed, we dreamed, we schemed.
We ruled the streets of Chicago, um hmm.
Now (hmm) we're here in the desert of Idaho, oh yeah.

Things are changin', things are changin'.
We're makin' it big, I'm gettin' big.
I'm making it real big, oh yeah.
Ya know, my heart belongs to Chicago,
but yeah, makin' it big here.
So, I gotta take a nap. Talk to all yous later.
Good night.

Chapter Fifteen: Love Sparks

Wrigley didn't know if Rush would understand and forgive him or not, but he sure hoped so. He knew, he just knew, that Rush Palmer was the right one for him, for the rest of his life. It only took the first date to come to this conclusion. She was the only one who understood him, the pain he had to grow up with because of the loss of his mother at such a young age.

After all, Rush had endured the same kind of grief. When she lost her dad, she felt as if the only way to prevent any further unbearable pain related to love was to numb and ignore the sensation if it ever crept into her life again—well, with the exception of the rest of her family. And even the capacity to love her family had been damaged, too.

The South-Sider, Wrigley, changed all that one day when Rush hopped down the alleyway to meet her mother after work from her second job. Sometimes Rush even volunteered there, too, at Rabbi's Bunny and Hare Club, an evening sports program for lesser advantaged rabbits in the South side neighborhood. As they tried to hop home, Caponey and the rest of the South-Siders were there to harass them. They were making fun of their fur, the way they hopped, the way they talked. Called them haughty high-class rich, wiggle-waggle-nosed hares. It wasn't the most serious kind of bullying, but very aggravating. They kept hopping in front of them and wouldn't let them get by.

Wrigley seemed to be the only one of the bunch that could convince Caponey to get the others to stop the nonsense. Mrs. Palmer wasn't going to quit working there and Wrigley stepped in so she didn't have to experience the grief as she hopped home from Rabbi's.

Rush thanked him. They took one look into each other's eyes and instantly felt a strong connection. But it sure got a lot more profound when, after three requests, Rush agreed to go for some carrot juice one day with her new admirer and the topic came up about the loss of their parents. Finally, someone understood Rush and vice versa. Wrigley connected to the gang, it was his only family, but with Rush he felt a goodness and kindness, a passion for life, a sense of right and wrong, and secretly hoped that some of her good qualities might rub off on him.

He figured he blew it, though, when he didn't hop on that train with her to Idaho. He just had to win her trust again. There was something else in his life now besides the gang and it felt right and good. He had to try.

When he finally found out where they were camping, Wrigley put his right paw to his lips as Ryker and the Arlingtons saw him coming their way. "Shhh," he whispered.

Rush had her back to him and was working on an entry in her journal. He tapped her on the shoulder. She shook the paw off, kept her head down and said, "Go away, Ryker, I'm trying to write here." Wrigley tapped her again and Rush snapped her head around, ready to yell at her brother, and exclaimed, "Wrigley! You came! You found us!"

She gave him a big hug. Boy did that feel good, he thought to himself.

Then suddenly, her demeanor changed. "Wait, what am I doing? You abandoned us, me and Ryker, just when we needed you. I don't want anything to do with you. If I ever fall in love, and I'm not saying that I will, it will be with someone who would give his life for me and my family. So you can just go right back to Chicago, Wrigley *Soxer*." She emphasized *Soxer*. She knew it wasn't his real last name, but that's what he always called himself, since he liked both the Cubs and White Sox.

"Rush, please, just listen to me for a minute. Just one minute of your time, okay? Then if you want me to leave, I will. I promise." He looked at her with pleading eyes.

"One minute? Sure. Time starts now. Go," she said matter-of-factly, not expecting to hear anything of value.

"I have a surprise for you." He grinned.

"What kind of surprise? If you think a ring is gonna change any—"

Wrigley cut her off. "No, Rush, it's your mom, she's here. Let me take you to her." He reached out for her paws.

"My mom? Really? You brought my mom here to N.J.R.C.?" She looked into his eyes and felt happier than she had in a long time.

"Yes, Rush. Listen, the only reason I didn't come with you is because the boss, Caponey, had this scatter-brained idea to kidnap your mom and use her to get the Mayor here to hand over some of the magic water. I knew what he was planning, but I couldn't stop him.

So I figured the best thing to do was to play along and stick with her. She's waiting for you and Ryker. C'mon!"

This time Rush took a hold of his paws and with tears in her eyes she hugged him and said the words he was hoping to hear from her someday. "Oh thank you, Wrigley, is she okay? I love you!" She surprised herself as the words rolled off her tongue.

The two melted into each other's arms. "She's fine, Rush, really. Anxious to see her kids though. And guess what?" he teased.

"What?"

"I love you, too, you cuddly, adorable, lovable rabbit. C'mon. Get your brother. Let's go."

"Okay!" She hugged him tightly again.

Rush's uncle and aunt stood there staring at them, smiling, and feeling grateful that somebody had gotten through to Rush and enabled her to love once again and let go of some of the pain and disappointment she'd harbored for so many years.

"C'mon Ryker, Auntie Annie, Uncle Harvey. This is Wrigley, my boyfriend, he's going to take us to see Mom." She gave her aunt a big smile.

"Wrigley, is it?" Mr. Arlington asked, offering to shake his paw.

Wrigley was about to shake when Ryker jumped in front of his uncle and said, as serious as a tornado warning, "Look, Wrigley, you hurt my Sis and it will be karate chops for you, you got it? I know she's all gaga over you, but…"

Rush yanked her little brother and pulled him aside. "Look, you little Muppet, I can take care of myself. Quit thinking you're my keeper. He's here, isn't he? He's gonna take us to Mom, now let's go." She gave him a pat on the head and a little shove forward.

But Ryker persisted. "Just remember, I'm watching you Wrigley gum smacker."

"Move it, Ryker. Go!" Rush gave him another little shove on his back.

Off they went to reunite with Mrs. Palmer who was waiting with frenzied anticipation. As the kids moved towards her, she didn't budge from the small fold-up camping chair she was resting in, but adjusted the colorful baby blanket Wrigley had given her to make sure her injured right leg was covered.

The reunion was a truly joyous, poignant moment, even if it was tainted by some emotional conflicts. After hugs and kisses, a firm reprimand from Mrs. Palmer to her kids followed, the usual, "Don't ever do that again, just run off like that." But she was just happy they were both safe and sound. She hadn't seen her sister in a long while either, so that was an added bonus, a positive thing that happened because of all the uprooting. And Brooklyn Palmer had to admit, even to Rush, the change felt wonderful, strange, but good.

"Mom," Rush let her guard down finally, showed her vulnerability. "Here's Wrigley again. He said he stayed behind just so he could come out and watch over you. That Caponey, he's the one with the stupid kidnapping plot. Wrigley wanted to help. I love him, Mom. I truly do." She hugged her mom and tears erupted for both mom and daughter.

Ryker said sarcastically, "Oh yuck! Any mushier and you guys would all be winning awards for a soap opera performance."

Rush ignored him and went on and on how her mom was just going to love it in New Jack Rabbit City. "Right Auntie Annie and Uncle Harvey?"

"Well," Mrs. Arlington said, "from what we've seen, the town does have potential, and it certainly is beautiful out here. Suppose we should all just take it one day at a time. Oh, it's so good to see you, Brookie!" She gave her younger sister a hug.

"Thanks, Sis, and you too, Harvey, for watching over them. I didn't worry as much once I knew you were with them."

"Did you meet the others yet, the Buckinghams?" Harvey said. "Ryker's got himself a new friend."

Ryker looked up at his mom and gave her a happy affirming smile.

"Good, Ryker! No, I haven't met them yet. I'm sure we'll all see each other at that race today, soon. It's quite a different life, that's for sure. I could get used to all this, I suppose." Brooklyn sounded sincere and content in her observation.

Rush gave her another hug. "Oh, Mom, I love you. You're the best."

"You're the best, too, sweetheart. Just remember though, no more running off. We talk over things and act as a family should. What do you say?"

"Sure, Mom."

"Mom, I missed you!" Ryker said. He put his head down and tried not to cry.

"I missed you, too, Son, I'm glad we're all together again, our family. Even you, Annie and Harvey, how's that knee of yours?"

"It's okay Brookie, hanging in there. Let's get going. Maybe we can find that other family, the Buckinghams, and what about those South-Siders we keep hearing about? Wrigley, Son, I suppose they're like family to you. We all sure hope you have some ways of persuasion with them. N.J.R.C. is such a peaceful place. Nobody needs to be turning it into a crime or war zone." He stared at Wrigley like a father would to his own real live son during a heart-to-heart.

Wrigley stared right back. "Don't worry, I think Caponey's comin' around. The Mayor's been workin' on him. I think he even said he'd help out with the big chase. C'mon all you, follow me." Wrigley smiled and took Rush's paw. "We'll do a little visiting and then just see who is faster, hares or dogs. If I was a bettin' rabbit, which I'm not anymore," he glanced over to Mrs. Palmer, who still remained seated, "my money would sure be on the fast-track hares of N.J.R.C."

Rush and her mom looked at each other and laughed. "C'mon, Mom." Rush reached out her paw.

Mrs. Palmer tossed the baby blanket off to the ground, and Rush, Ryker, and the Arlingtons were shocked. "Mom, what happened?" both kids yelled out when they saw her right leg all bandaged up.

"Now, Rush, don't get upset. It was an accident. When Caponey told me to jump off the train, I hesitated a little. So Caponey told Wrigley to take my hand. I was so scared, I pulled back again as we were supposed to jump and slipped. Then I fell off instead of jumping. I got kind of scraped up and a sprain, but it's all healing now." She limped forward, holding onto Rush's right arm and wincing with every step. Clearly, her leg still hurt.

In an instant, Wrigley knew what was coming next.

"This is how you took care of my mom? Dragged her off a train and mangled her leg! See, this is what I told you a long time ago. Leave that stupid gang of yours or bad things would keep happening. You're more loyal to them then any of my family. I can't trust you, Wrigley, and I don't want anything else to do with you! You can forget what I said!" Rush wanted to run away, fast, but she had to hang onto her mom.

"But, Rush... I only tried to help. You just said you loved me. I love you." Wrigley hoped to get back on track with the loving connection they'd just professed.

"I don't want to hear it. Just go away. Leave us alone!"

"Yeah, Soxer," Ryker chimed in, "you're still nothing but trouble for my sis and my mom. Get lost!" He took a couple steps toward the disheartened hare.

Wrigley, who knew it was useless, for now anyway, just hopped away. It was faster than walking upright.

"Honey, he truly was trying to help," Mrs. Palmer said.

The Arlingtons spoke up, too, trying to reassure their niece. "You know, Rush, love is a precious thing. You two seem to really care for each other." They hopped slowly alongside of Rush, Ryker and their mom.

"Thanks, but no thanks. He's just trouble. I don't need the grief. C'mon, Ryker, let's go see your friend and the rest of the Buckinghams. And that race between the hares and dogs sounds like fun. I'll be okay. Don't worry about me," Rush said in a sincere and confident voice.

She couldn't wait to write this all down in her journal. Besides, she had learned all about solitude and had gotten used to it. No gangster rabbit was going to come along and mess up the way she had learned to survive and feel strong. Love, she thought: what a pain.

Mrs. Palmer was worried for her daughter, as usual, but she was sure glad to be back with her kids, knowing they were safe.

Chapter Sixteen: The Chase

As the truck swept between sage-covered hills and tumbleweeds stacked five-feet high on the guardrails, an array of transmitter dishes appeared in the shadow of a small gulley just to our right. The dishes at this latitude seem to often point southeast, straining at the sky for signals broadcast from orbiting satellites in the distant space. The site of these enormous towers broke the silence between the three of us.

"Just think," Abby said, "if these frequencies were not spinning through the air and the rabbits' ears didn't act like sensitive antennae, those jackrabbits would just be giant mutants running through the dunes at the State Park. They would have the magic spring and be six-feet-tall but be just as plain as the rabbits people buy at pet stores around Easter time."

"This brings me to another question," I said. "You know, I've only seen one big jackrabbit, the Mayor – have you seen any others?"

"Oh yeah," she answered quickly. "They're all over the place. Whenever we're in New Jack Rabbit City, I can feel their eyes watching our every move. They blend into the brush; their images mirror the surroundings. For millions of years they've survived in a hostile environment, and they had to adapt or become extinct. In this city of jacks they've taken it one step further. The spring water here can make their appearance almost translucent. Sometimes, I look right at them and see right through them; I see sage or sand, but not the rabbit. Other times, there they are, as real as can be. It's just like what happens in magical dreams."

I had to ask, "Where do you get these words from, Abby, like *translucent?*"

"From my advanced spelling bee word lists, of course."

The turn to the State Park came up quickly. An arrow and the words: "Bruneau State Park, highest sand dune in North America," were displayed on an aging sign on our left. The sun brutalizes all things painted on metal in this desert land and it was obvious that elements of nature had decayed the sign. Hikers, kite-fliers, and sand dune surfers greeted our eyes as we rolled up to our campsite.

"What do we do about those cowboys and that truck which is gonna drain the magic spring?" Zach asked as the truck came to a dusty halt just off the asphalt.

"We gotta let the Mayor know as soon as we see him." Abby spoke with even more determination than usual.

"I hope he doesn't cancel the chase," Zach said. "I know the dogs really want to race those rabbits and I wanna see them win!"

"It's not our decision," Abby snapped back, more like an adult than child. She gets this attitude when facing a crisis, I thought to myself. Tunnel vision in an eight year old can be scary. The temperature was already 89 degrees, and the plan was to pack some snacks, a few bottles of water, several dog treats, and head out to New Jack Rabbit City.

"Hey, let me lead," Zach proclaimed, "I got the map!" He opened the truck's front door, rubbed a hand across the dash, and looked concerned. He checked the floor, seats, between the seats, under the seats. Then he said in a distressed voice, "It's gone!"

"What is?" I asked.

"The map to New Jack Rabbit City! It was there, honest! I put it right on the dash, I'm sure of it."

"Positive, dead sure?" Abby jumped in.

"Yeah, no doubt," Zach answered firmly.

Then, as if a fortune teller at a traveling carnival, Abby calmly said, "Stolen in town, I bet, maybe by those cowboys, or the two rabbits Eggy chased." Then she started lecturing us. "We are coming to a crossroads, the very existence of the benevolent hares and the influence of evil intent just like Mr. Mayor talked about—that greed versus goodness."

Zach rolled his eyes again at me as he does sometimes. I just gave him a quick smile and nod. He'd confided in me one day how he gets tired of his little sister always acting so smart, especially since he's the older one. Zach reminded me that he gets good grades in school, too, saying, "I'm just not a show-off, like she is."

I assured the kids we could find our way to N.J.R.C. again, no problem. So, with Eggy well-rested and Nache (Nasty's name when he's behaving himself) looking like the rock face of El Capitan in Yosemite National Park with his yellow lab characteristics, we headed out.

The five of us cruised over the dunes, through the sagebrush, followed a faint trail past the first lake and beach to the intriguing *Jack Rabbits Only* sign. Under the archway of hemlock trees we entered, once again, into the magical wonderland.

Abby said, "I can feel the eyes watching us," so I opened my eyes wide and turned my head very slowly, first in one direction and then the other. Yes, I could feel it, within the trees, the brush, the sand itself. I felt watched. Within seconds, there he stood, right in front of us, Mr. Mayor.

"I am glad you made it back. Our city is looking forward to a good chase with those dogs of yours. Swale and Ruffian have been loosening up all morning. Swale and Ruffian are names of racehorses in case you didn't know. When we first picked up the frequencies, the Kentucky Derby and other horse races fascinated us, so the fastest of our young hares got these names, maybe odd to you, but a tradition here. Seabisk, we shortened his name just a bit, is another favorite. He couldn't make it today; he's tending to a slight sprain. Follow me," he concluded the conversation, and strode off in the direction of a clearing just over a small dune and through a teacup-shaped depression.

I gave Abby a tap on her back, so she quickly ran up to him and shouted, "Wait, stop, Mr. Mayor! I have something very important to tell you!" She leaned into his left eight-inch-long ear and informed him, "We heard some gossip in town this morning, Your Honor. Someone else knows about your magic spring and wants the water all to themselves. A couple of cowboys have got a huge tanker truck and monster pump and they said they are coming out here to 'suck this spring dry.' They looked dead serious and were taking orders from some big-shot rancher. They're meeting at the old slaughterhouse at 5 P.M. tomorrow." Abby sighed and took a few deep breaths.

The Mayor's face remained calm. He brushed back one of his giant ears and thanked Abby for her concern. He also looked over at me and nodded.

Then he looked into Abby's eyes and reassured her, "Don't you worry child. We can be six-feet-tall and upright or have all four paws on the ground, but we will always survive. We have for thousands of years. We have faced every threat nature and man has thrown at us in the past; we will figure out a plan to survive this little hiccup. Let me put on my thinking cap and talk with my advisors. We'll figure out how do deal with this. But we won't let this get in the way of the sporting event we have planned for today. My young hares are ready to give those dogs of yours a run they will never forget."

We started walking again and as he pushed back a few tree limbs, I got my first look at the arena. I was amazed. It was similar to the obstacle course we saw before, but this one was more extensive. It sported curved runways, walls, banked rows of planked timbers, jumps feet off the ground, single rails suspended on wooden blocks.

"WOW!" I knelt down with one knee in the sand, Eggy on my left, Nasty to the right, their tongues sticking out, tails dancing. "What do you think boys?" I asked aloud. Both of my excited dogs replied with a lick to my cheek.

There it was, the course laid out in front of us. The series of obstacles and runs intrigued not only us – the dogs also had a look of surprise. This was not going to be an ordinary (dog chases a rabbit up a sand dune) kind of race. This obstacle course had some cool challenges for both competitors.

The Mayor spoke loudly with a microphone so all the gathered hares and rabbits could hear. First he had to settle the crowd down. I did not want to call it a rabble, but what else was it? Imagine a hundred or more rabbits and hares standing upright in the middle of a desert in the shadow of a monstrous sand dune lined up all around an obstacle course and shouting at one another. The yelling even shook the sagebrush sprouting up in long hedges surrounding the natural arena.

Many were shaking some kind of paperwork or currency in the faces of each other and acting very determined to make a point. A couple of tall, lean rabbits sure did look as if they were playing the role of "bookies."

Those attending had no fashion sense. There were some in mismatched suits, black shirts with brown pants, stripes blending with dotted ties, and the colors: reds and bright blues, purple scarves, and top hats in black and white. American flags and "Be Kind to Animals" pins draped many lapels. All of the bold colors were in stark contrast to the backdrop grey-colored landscape. The younger hares had rock band T-shirts and wore jeans in keeping with their human counterparts. Some were naked, yes, just regular hares standing around in their natural fur coats. Some large, six-feet or so, many still small, but they had one thing in common: even though many hares at the chase event had funny-looking big feet, almost twice the size as other hares or pictures I'd seen, all wore some kind of footwear—shoes and sneakers, slip-ons, and Indian moccasins even adorned their unique feet.

I looked upward and was glad it didn't look like rain, even though a few clouds hovered above. I heard the Mayor tapping on the microphone and knew the chase was about to start.

"Today we have a meet between these two fine dogs, Eggy and Nasty, and our finest hares on the course, Swale and Ruffian. For the benefit of our human and canine friends, I will explain the competition. There will be three heats, two between one hare and one dog, the finale, being a rare tandem run through the maze. If one of our hares is touched by one of the dogs, the round goes to the dogs. If the rabbit is untouched, round goes to the rabbit. The rabbits get a one yard head start. They follow the course and the dogs chase them. Is that clear?"

He turned to me as I was kneeling down with the dogs straddling my sides. I looked over to Eggy and Nasty, then gave the Mayor the thumbs up. Abby and Zach gave the dogs one last good-luck pet before they headed for the sidelines.

The large amphitheater, sitting like a giant bowl between sand dunes, was a buzz of excitement. Many of the large and small rabbits and hares hopped or walked up to us and tried to size up the competing dogs. The long legs and athletic build of Eggy garnered some long stares from many of the jacks. Nasty, with his superiority complex, just rolled his eyes at their scrutiny.

I studied the course the dogs would be facing: a start in sand, about fifty feet, then on to a banked track of boards, over a short wall, under a three foot bridge, and into the sand again, this time a longer stretch, around two turns, then the finish line.

Eggy would go first, since he would never settle for second. Ruffian approached the starting line, all rabbit muscle, big in the thighs, lean in the front paws, this hare could lift some major weight. But could he match Eggy's four-foot strides?

The chase was about to begin. The Mayor, in a very official capacity, lifted his arms and shouted out, "Ladies and gentle hares and our human friends, welcome to the chase! Okay hare and dog, up to the line! When my arm goes down it is off to the races. The first round matches the canine Eggy with our Ruffian. Does your dog understand the rules?" He looked directly at Eggy.

Both dogs looked up at me. "Yes," I replied for them. With a quick jerk, Eggy's head faced forward and he acted like he couldn't wait to start running as fast as he could. "You boys chase down the rabbit, touch him and we win. Got it, Eggy? You're up first. Nasty, you stay!" I held on to his collar, just to make sure.

"You only wish it will be that easy! You ain't gonna win nothin'!" came a shout from somewhere in the crowd. The bantering brought a loud laugh from the spectators.

Eggy glanced at me as if he was ready to sprint. Ruffian nodded to the hometown crowd who cheered at his gesture as they waited in the starting blocks. The Mayor dropped his hand and in a sand storm they were off. In the first twenty feet of the chase Eggy had the advantage, with his long legs and a horse-like stride, even though some jackrabbits and hares have enormous rear legs, themselves.

The power turn is the strength of hares in a chase, and on the planks Eggy started losing ground. Ruffian hit the first turn flying, his jumbo rear legs hitting the bank and springing into a three-yard lead. But Eggy lengthened his stride, zoomed into a higher speed, and moved closer along the runways between the turns. Ruffian's lead shrunk to just inches and he must have felt Eggy breathing down his back.

At the jump, over a two-foot wall, Ruffian went airborne, and Eggy followed his flight. The hare, a lot lighter, landed smoothly, but Eggy hit hard, so the hare's lead lengthened. Three more turns and to the final straightaway and the first race would be over. Eggy pushed harder and, learning fast, began leveraging his lean body into the turns. Back to a nine-inch lead, the crowd roared, and chants of "Ruffian, Ruffian, Ruffian" exploded from the sidelines. I was sure the noise from the crowd could be heard all the way to the Snake River.

The final straightaway was Eggy's last hope to catch his challenger. Ruffian entered it with three feet between them. Eggy pushed it to the limit; the hare still sprinted in full stride. Ruffian put his head down and, literally, by the length of half his right ear, won the finish. Race one had gone to Ruffian, and the spectators loved it.

Eggy trotted over to me, and with a big hug and a kiss on the nose I told him, "It's okay, big boy, it's okay. Good dog."

The cheering continued long after the finish. Ruffian did a half lap, to the delight of his cheering audience.

"Race One to the hare!" The Mayor moved back into the spotlight. "Let's prepare for Race Two. This heat has the canine Nasty and our own Swale."

Swale, like his counterpart, showed great strength in his back legs and had slightly longer ears than his racing partner. Nasty, smaller and younger than Eggy, didn't have the long strides like his brother Lab, but he possessed good sprinting speed. Although I love my Eggy, Nasty is the schemer, smart as a fox. It's almost as if he watched the first race, because he acted so self-confidently, as if he had a plan.

The Mayor brought the two competitors to the starting line, raised his front paw, dropped it, and they were off.

Swale hit the boards full tilt. So did Nasty, who slowed down just enough to get the traction he needed to bounce into the banked turn, his smaller size a better suit for the sharp swerves of this obstacle course. He inched closer. Swale must have sensed this, so he raced even faster and gained eighteen inches. Nasty had concocted a plan, I thought to myself. The hurdle came up and the hare went flying. Nasty spun right, passed just left of the jump, cut across twenty feet of open ground, and entered the next planked straightaway, just as the hare raced full speed ahead. Not looking back, Nasty grabbed five strands of furry tail.

Race Two over. The boos exploded. Nasty, with hare fur still in his mouth, taunted the crowd as he pranced around and did a victory lap, too. His opponent seemed stunned. Nobody knew what to think. Many just felt as if Nasty had not run a fair race. Even I wondered if, perhaps, he might be disqualified.

The Mayor, sensing the hostility, raised both his paws to the sky and the crowd got quiet. "There is only one rule in this contest and we all know it, DOG CHASES HARE. Nasty outsmarted Swale. It's a lesson for all of us—'one eye forward, one eye always looking back.' Congratulations, Nasty, on winning Race Two."

I could see in the crowd the same currency or paperwork as before changing hands again. Some wise jacks had picked up on the mischief in Nasty's eyes and made the right gamble. (I found out later from the Mayor, though, that all the bets were over vegetables and trade services, not actual money. Said he wouldn't have any part of that, but he had hares who still tried.)

After the dogs and hares lapped up their drinking water and enjoyed a couple of treats, the Mayor stepped up to the starting line for the last time.

"Are the hares ready?" He turned to Ruffian and Swale, who were now flanked by several other hares who looked like part of their training staff. A tall athletic built hare sporting an Adidas warm-up suit, gave a thumbs up.

The Mayor continued, "This is the tandem chase. The pathways have been widened, two dogs, two hares, any dog touches hare and the race is over. This is the deciding race. Good luck to all!"

Swale and Ruffian moved up to the line and both looked confident. Eggy and Nasty appeared fresh even after their first runs. Both stretched and took to their starting spot thirty six inches behind the hares. The Mayor, for the third and final time, lifted up his paws and then let them fall.

All four skidded into a burn-out and caused sand to fly into the faces of several jacks too close to the action. Just as before, the dogs closed fast in the first straightaway. Into the first wooden turn, Eggy remained just inches from Swale. We could hear the sound of paws on planks echoing through the hollow. Both dogs were panting hard and racing into turn two. Eggy was gaining ground.

Out of the turn, now with just one hare tail separating them and the straightaway coming up in twenty, Eggy was going to get a mouth full of fur if nothing changed. But Nasty seemed to have another action plan, as if he knew they would be watching for his trick play. Coming to the point where he peeled off last time, he jerked in that direction but didn't really turn. Ruffian, waiting for his ploy, power-turned to the opposite side. Eggy had just opened his mouth for the sweet taste of victory – the furry tail – but the turn brought nothing into his mouth but sand and air.

With the two foot wall just three feet away, both hares jumped into space, flew together and remained in flight as Eggy lifted his ninety pounds into the air. Nasty made a snap decision – he dodged to the right, avoided the jump, and lunged forward to catch Swale on his landing, but his timing was a little late and in the wrong spot.

It looked as if Eggy spotted Nasty, but in mid-air and traveling very fast, his options were limited. I watched the collision as if it happened in slow motion. Eggy landed right on the back of Nasty. His weight smashed Nasty into the sand, and Eggy, with his head and tail spinning end-over-end through the air, landed butt-first in the sand. He flipped back on his feet, but it was too late. Ruffian and Swale were ten feet from the finish. Eggy, a champion at heart, got right back up and sprinted after them to the finish line. Swale and Ruffian crossed the line with paws raised to the sky, to the cheers of the hometown crowd.

Nasty stayed down. I knew what it meant: he'd either play hurt, as he does sometimes, or finish the race like his big brother, Eggy, and this was him playing hurt. He picked up his back paw and limped across the race course back to me. That's my Nasty, and that's exactly how he got his name.

The cheers continued. Swale and Ruffian took their victory spin around the course. Zach and Abby ran over to me and the dogs. With my arms around both Eggy and Nasty, I petted them both and whispered in their ears a couple times, "Good dogs, good dogs," and the chase was over.

Zach was disappointed that the dogs didn't win, but Abby set him straight. "They did their best, Zach. It's just about running in the race and trying, not always about winning." I smiled at Abby for her young wisdom.

Zach perked up, hugged the dogs and whispered in their ears, too. "Good dogs, good dogs."

THE CHASE

Now listen up, all you young hare fans out there.
We're The Rappin' Rabbits and we got somethin'
we want to share.

Life's about the chase, not losses or gains.
Life's all about participatin', enjoyin' the games.
That's right, that's right, it's all about life.
That's right, it's all about the game called life.

You gotta keep chasin', you gotta keep chasin'.
You gotta keep racin', you gotta keep racin'.
You gotta keep chasin', you gotta keep chasin'.
You gotta keep racin', you gotta keep racin'.

Chase life fast, chase life slow.
But chase it hard, chase it long.
It's the only way to go.

Rabbits, dogs, humans, they can all run the race.
But it's not about the finish line.
It's all about the chase.
It's not about the finish line, it's all about the chase.

Finish lines are fine, just fine, give closure,
add reason and rhyme.
But it's not about the finish line,
it's all about the chase.
That's right, it's all about the chase.

When life gets you down,
you're wearin' that frown,
it's no time to give up, quit clownin' around.
Gotta believe in tomorrows, tone down your sorrows.
Put a smile on your face.
Get back in the race.

You gotta keep chasin', you gotta keep chasin'.
You gotta keep racin', you gotta keep racin'.
You gotta keep chasin', you gotta keep chasin'.
You gotta keep racin', you gotta keep racin'.

If the cards are stacked against you,
buy another deck of cards and reach for the stars.
No matter, no matter, who you are.
That's what ya do, that's what ya do.
If the cards are stacked against you,
ya buy another deck of cards, that's what ya do.
That's what you do.

Reachin' destinations is tough.
Journeys are rough.
But keep chasin', it's good for the soul.
As long as you keep chasin',
you can rock and roll.

You gotta keep chasin', keep chasin' toward a new start.
Gotta believe it, gotta believe it, right smack dab in the heart.
It's all about the chase. It's all about the chase.
Keep chasin'. Keep chasin'.

Chapter Seventeen: Slaughterhouse at Five

Mr. Mayor and the advisory council met late in the evening after the exciting chase to discuss the Bossy Kincaid situation. Their action plan? Thanks to Abby's warning, they knew the time that Bossy and his drivers would meet at the old meatpacking warehouse.

Mr. Mayor didn't trust too many humans who came to town, but sure did appreciate the warning, and he liked this family a lot. Abby and Zach, even the big guy – the Mayor thought they were like those folks in the movie *E.T.* (That was another discovery and human-type enjoyment for the new generation of rabbits, television. *E.T.* and *Alice and Wonderland* were two of their favorite movies.) Even though the rabbits could talk and many were tall now and looked different, the family didn't see them as alien creatures to fear. They simply accepted them and tried to get to know them; so they were considered trustworthy friends.

The Mayor took the lead as usual, said he'd be there and try to talk some sense into the selfish "don't have a clue" bandits. He'd offer them a jug of magic water and explain, or try to, that it doesn't do a thing for cows or dogs who lap up the water—or any other animals, just rabbits.

He wasn't naïve, though. Mr. Mayor and all the rest of his advisors knew they had their paws full with the Chicago egotistical gangster, Caponey, and now they were dealing with foolish, greedy men from outside of N.J.R.C. who wanted to vacuum up all the wells bone dry and trample all over the beautiful dunes and New Jack Rabbit City with their big rig.

Bossy Kincaid's slaughterhouse had remained empty ever since some fool thought a couple sick cows meant Mad Cow disease and sounded the alarm. Rumors spread and that's all it took. The owner sanitized and disinfected it over and over, but once it was emptied out, none of the local ranchers wanted to risk sending their cattle there. Even Bossy knew he'd lose money if he tried to put any cows back in that old plant.

The huge, haunted-house-like structure sits on an old railroad siding location surrounded by weeds. Railroad ties continue to split in the hot sun, and much of the metal holding the rails in place has been scavenged by locals to sell as scrap. It reeks of foul odors: scents of leftover sun-baked beer, wine, and rotting hay. Pigeons fill the sky when disturbed by intruders, and the slapping of their wings breaks the eerie silence.

Now it provides a hideout for romping young rabbits, teen lovers from Mountain Home, and, of course, serves as the perfect hangout for underage drinkers and pot-smokers. Along with the distinct aroma of marijuana—empty beer and wine bottles are stacked up in the corners. Occasionally, rats dart between the Miller Lite cans, Boone's Farm, and other wine receptacles. The inside of the deserted building feels and looks like a B-Movie soundstage: dreary and unsavory.

It was here on the day after the big chase, right on schedule at five 'til five in the afternoon, as the plan to raid N.J.R.C.'s magic water supply grew closer, that Bossy Kincaid chugged down more than a few shots of whiskey. It made him feel a lot stronger, braver. Wiley and Casey, they kept showing their furry arm muscles to Bossy, assuring him that they were well-equipped and would fight to the end if needed. Wiley, especially, he wasn't leaving N.J.R.C. without that water so he could grow big and strong once and for all. Oh, and get rich, too.

Kincaid and his drivers had their weapons all loaded and set to go: a rifle placed right in the middle of the two cowboys, and one set on Bossy's dashboard. They even had a bow and arrow in the back of his pickup. They figured that would do it.

Bossy shared his sentiments with Wiley and Casey. "How could them stupid rabbits even think they could fight us off with all the ammunition we got here?"

But the intruders would find out soon enough that Mr. Mayor meant it when he'd assured everyone that he had some tricks up his sleeves. (Whenever he wore flashy, colorful clothes, anyway.) N.J.R.C. rabbits had their ways of fighting evil. Bossy and all the rest would find that out, for sure.

Mr. Mayor had a hunch about Caponey, too. He still kept drinking the magic water, growing in size, and talking about going back and ruling the streets of Chicago. But if the Mayor's hunch was right, Caponey was basically a lazy fellow who mostly fed off feeling like he had power and respect from his followers. If the South-Sider "rumble" against the intruders could make Caponey look and feel like a major "good-guy" player during the altercation, and he came through and helped the Mayor and others win the battle, so to speak, then Caponey might change his ways and want to go right on doing good things and keep feeling good about himself.

So there they were: Bossy, Wiley, Casey, the two drivers who liked to dress up like John Wayne, cowboy boots and all, with their tanker truck loudly idling away. Ready, in a heartbeat, to cause all kinds of havoc that the Mayor was there to prevent, if possible.

In an instant, Mr. Mayor made himself visible.

Chuck, one of the drivers spoke up. "Well, lookie here, what do we have 'hare,' the real thing? The true livin' six-feet-tall funny-dressed rabbit we've all been hearin' about, right here before our eyes."

Bossy Kincaid, on his way to being drunk as usual, standing right beside his two drivers along with his partners, Wiley and Casey, in a quest for the magic water, blurted out: "Just shoot him! Get him outta the way boys!"

But they didn't. Instead, the Mayor said calmly, "Well hello there, Mister Kincaid, boys, and fellow hares. Just a moment of your time, that's all I'd like."

Kincaid stared into the Mayor's eyes and said, "We got nothin' to say to you. Nothin' you can say to my boys here. We're goin' in and tappin' that well o' yours. C'mon, boys, let's go! Just use that rifle o' yours if he won't move out."

"Now hold on a minute there. I'm here to make life a whole lot easier for all of us. You don't have to charge in here and trample over our beautiful dunes and city with your monster truck or start waving any weapons around. I've got some water for you right here in this jug. I give you my word, as Mayor of N.J.R.C., that this is the real thing, a sample of the water you're looking for. All I'm asking is that you take it to one of your cows and try it. Or bring one of your cows here. I'll let it drink right from the spring. You'll see for yourself that the water does nothing, absolutely nothing, to cows. Rabbits and hares are the only animals I've ever witnessed who are affected by it. Are you hearing me?" The Mayor gave them all an impatient, scornful look. "Oh, we've heard a few rumors about some talking raccoons, but I've yet to confirm that."

Chuck looked at his partner, Jeff. Wiley looked at Casey. Bossy looked at all of them looking at each other and said, "Just shoot him! Are you buyin' this double talk?"

All four of them shook their heads no.

Bossy continued, "You ain't foolin' any of us with that bunch of baloney double talk. What you think we are, stupid hick farmers or somethin'? Well we ain't. Yeah, we're farmers, but sophistercatin' businessmen, too. Now you can just go back and tell all your hares, six-foot or not, to stay outta our way. 'Cause we're comin' in and we're getting' us that water!" After he finished his speech, he went into a coughing fit.

Chuck and Jeff spit out some tobacco chew and chimed in, "Yeah!"

In the midst of the confrontation, Wiley hopped right up to the Mayor and said, "I'll be happy to take that jug of water from ya, real pleased, if you'd like to hand it over." He never stopped dreaming of growing tall just like the miracle giant-sized rabbit standing before him. He started licking his lips.

Bossy got his breath back and yelled at him, "Wiley, get your furry butt over here! We ain't takin' no measly little jug of water. We'll be takin' it all. Every last drop! You got that, giant-ears?"

Mr. Mayor stood with his arms crossed. "So you're telling me there is no reasoning with you on this matter, even though all your tactics and greediness may disrupt our town for nothing?"

"Yeah, that's what I'm tellin' ya, big guy." Bossy crossed his arms, too, turned to Chuck and Jeff and added, "Ain't that so, boys?"

They both looked into Bossy's bloodshot eyes and noticed his body swaying from left to right as if he was about ready to fall down.

"Bossy, maybe it's true," Jeff attempted to talk to him. "Maybe…"

"It's all lies! Ya hear me, all lies! He just don't want us takin' his precious magic water." Bossy turned back to the Mayor again but neither he nor the water jug were anywhere in sight. "Where'd that lousy, lyin' giant go to?" He staggered forward to look for him, almost fell over, turned to Chuck and said, "I need a drink. Wiley, get me my bottle, will ya, from the front seat of my pickup. Use those workin' gloves I got there on the dash if ya have to. Then we're goin' in. You're with me, all o' you, right? Ain't no double talkin' giant hare gonna keep us from gettin' rich." He slobbered and tried to wipe it away with his sleeve.

Wiley was all for it. He couldn't wait for super-sized cows to make him rich and to grow big himself. Chuck, Jeff, and Casey, just a bunch of followers, usually did whatever Bossy ordered and paid them to do. They didn't dream near as big as Wiley.

Chuck laughed. "Okay, Boss. Your call. We gotta wait just a little while, though. A buddy of mine told me we should wait 'til them two park rangers who work here everyday clear out. Then we'll rock and roll. Hey, we can call ourselves The Desert Stormers!"

Wiley ran back in with Bossy's whiskey bottle. "Here ya go, Boss. So are we goin' in?" His eyes widened with excitement.

"Yeah, we're goin' in. Real soon, real soon. Chuck says we gotta wait for a couple of rangers to leave. Let's me, you and Casey go jump in my truck. When we head in, we'll follow Chuck and Jeff since they got the tanker. I gave them the map. Almost time to get rich, kids." Bossy laughed and sported his devilish grin.

Casey was just glad to get out of that slaughterhouse. It gave him the shivers. He mumbled "jeepers, creepers" when he arrived and once again as he hopped out. "Jeepers, creepers." The eerie old meatpacking warehouse had a deadly, sordid past.

Within minutes, Bossy fell asleep and snored like a human with one nostril plugged up and wheezed like he had bronchial tubes the size of tiny straws. The others sat there, waiting and thinking, while Wiley mostly daydreamed.

Chapter Eighteen: Back in New Jack Rabbit City

If it wasn't the contrary Caponey the Mayor and the rest of N.J.R.C. were dealing with, it was the crazy, nonsensical get-rich scheme of Kincaid and his cowboys wanting to plow a tanker truck right into town and disrupt the harmony even more.

Following the excitement of the big race, as more and more of the hares and rabbits heard about the threats to their peaceful town and Bossy Kincaid's scheme, they all wanted to help any way they could, of course. Even Caponey had surprised himself by developing an affection for N.J.R.C. and started thinking hard about how he could crush them cowboys and that Kincaid fellow with one foot, now that he was getting so gosh darn big.

Everybody had heard about the kids and Mike warning the Mayor and the way the family left right after the big chase event. Mike and the Mayor thought it was best if the kids went on home and tried to reassure everyone that, although there was some trouble coming, it wouldn't be long before all was taken care of and N.J.R.C. would return to the peaceful, amazing wonderland they had all enjoyed. There was just something special about the Mayor, so almost everybody trusted him.

Zach surprised the Mayor and begged his Uncle Mike not to go home. He'd told them both that he was going to "stay and fight to the death" just like he'd witnessed on his warrior video games. But again, the Mayor offered reassurance, insisting on the family's departure and telling Zach that while his courage was admirable, he didn't think, and certainly hoped, that "fighting to the death" would not really be necessary.

Mrs. Palmer, the Buckinghams and Arlingtons, they were worried sick—they sure didn't want any kids getting run over by some huge tanker or their husbands getting caught up in the turmoil. The Mayor tried to set everyone's mind at ease, promised that things would be okay, and asked everyone to trust him. Said he might need their help, but just trust him.

In N.J.R.C., as they sat talking, Ryker bugged his mom about the possibility of joining the ranks of Mr. Mayor's protectors, the Rabbit Patrol Guards, for the oncoming confrontation. After all, he had special-made slingshots all ready to go, and Bobbiteer to team up with. (Ryker loved nunchucks, but hadn't adapted or mastered them yet.)

"Now Ryker, you've been warned like the rest of us, stay back out of sight, since we haven't had enough of the one water formula that helps us to become invisible yet," Brooklyn reminded her son. "After all, they'll probably have guns. The Mayor seems to know what he is doing. Let's just follow his lead for any war battles that might occur." She used her most convincing parental voice, hoping he would listen.

Miranda Buckingham felt the same way and said so to Bobbiteer. "We did not come here from the city to engage in war! Son, I don't want you anywhere near that meatpacking warehouse or those bad guys, do you hear me?"

What else could he say but, "Yes, Mom, I hear you." He thought at least she could have said it when Ryker wasn't around. He felt better, though, since Ryker's mom had made him promise to be careful, too. Secretly, deep down, all Ryker and his new friend, Bobbit, could think about was loading up their slingshots, fighting the enemies, and protecting their families.

"See, Mom, I hate it here. I hate it! We're out of the city and where'd we end up? In this messed-up place, just another battleground. Well, if we can't go be soldiers, can we at least go to the beach?" Bobbit asked, looking up at his mom with pleading eyes.

"Hmm. To the beach? Right. Sure, Son, you can go to the beach, as long as your father goes with you." Miranda glanced over to Wyndhameer. Their eyes met and he knew exactly what she was doing: not trusting her son and making sure a parent stayed close by, so Bobbit would not disobey her orders. What she didn't know, though, was that her husband and Harvey Arlington both had every intention of taking off and helping out the Mayor and the other rabbits and hares of N.J.R.C. as much as they could. They were men, after all, older men, but men.

As long as Wyndhameer and Harvey were going, Brooklyn agreed to let Ryker go, too. "But you and Bobbiteer both stay within sight of Mr. Buckingham and Mr. Arlington. Got it?"

"Yes, Mom, I got it. Bye. See ya later."

Just as the four of them hopped off toward the beach, Rush saw them leave, stopped writing in her journal and asked her mom, "Where are they all going?"

"Oh, they're just going to the beach for a while. Were you writing some poetry or something in that journal of yours?" Brooklyn asked and smiled.

"No. If you must know, I was writing how stupid love is. First it's love. Then it's break up. Or, you think you're gonna live your whole life with someone you love and something bad happens and he dies." Rush quickly realized how her comments might be very painful for her mother to hear.

"Yes, Rush. Things happen. But you know what? Life goes on. And if you think for one second that your dad would want you to give up on love, or even me, if I get the chance to love again – I'm not an old rabbit, you know – then you didn't know you're father at all. He told me once: 'Love is the only thing in life that matters. Without love, there is nothing, nothing in this world worth anything.' Those are your dad's words, not mine, sweetheart."

Rush hung her head down. She placed both her paws over her teary eyes, took a hop forward toward her mom, uncovered her eyes, looked up and said, "I'm sorry, Mom. I just wanted to come here so we could all be happier. Nothing's working though. Nothing."

"Time, my dear, time. Time is like magic. One day it can be so dark, so painful. The next day the sun is shining and there's nothing but joy and happiness in your heart and soul. But, believe me, if your heart is not filled with hope and love, the dark days might just take over. So be careful." She stroked the flannel baby blanket Wrigley had given her that was now covering her legs.

"How's your leg, Mom?" Rush managed a smile.

"Better, much better, think I'll be hopping around normal as can be real soon."

When Wyndhameer, Harvey, Bobbiteer, and Ryker reached an intersection in the dunes, one pathway leading to the beach, one leading to the springhouse, the kids thought they were making a wrong turn.

"Ugh, Dad, the beach is this way," Bobbiteer said as he pointed.

"I know, Son. But we're not going that way. Now listen, Harvey and I have talked about this and we've decided to go help the Mayor and others. We could tell you both to head for the beach and not follow, but we know you won't do that. As long as you listen to us and do as we say, you're coming with us. Do you understand? You stand where we say. You do what we tell you to. Understood?" Wyndhameer gave them both a stern look.

"You mean we're gonna get to be soldiers after all? Oh man, Ryker, can you believe this? Oh yeah, Dad, yeah, we'll do whatever you say," Bobbiteer promised his dad as he swung his slingshot up in the air a few times.

"Thanks, Uncle Harvey," Ryker said. "We'll do whatever you say. Promise. Cross my heart," and then he crossed his heart.

Bobbiteer and Ryker lined up behind the two older hares and let them lead the way. "We're right behind you. Lead the way," they both chimed in.

The two youngsters looked at each other and didn't say another word. But the surprise in their eyes said it all. They couldn't believe what was happening. They were headed for battle! That's how they felt about it, anyway.

When the kids and husbands did not return within a reasonable amount of time, the worrying began back in N.J.R.C. Ryker's mom, Brooklyn, and Harvey's wife, Annie, instinctively knew that something was wrong. Rush volunteered to go check at the beach to see if they were still there. Her mom suggested that she find Wrigley, too. Maybe some of the South-Siders could help if they hadn't all gone to the slaughterhouse. If Brooklyn Palmer wasn't still healing from her leg injury, she would have hopped right up and gone herself. But she knew Rush could find out what was going on a lot faster than her.

First, Rush checked the beach. Sure enough, she didn't even see any rabbit or hare prints. She scurried over to the South-Siders' campsite and found Wrigley and all the other gang members, except Caponey, sitting around in a circle discussing whether they should head for the old slaughterhouse or not. The Mayor had told the Chicago hares, as well as all of the other N.J.R.C. rabbits, except his Rabbit Patrol Guard Unit of ten, to stay put. He said they'd all have the capability of being invisible and could handle it. He did ask for Caponey's help because he had gotten so big, thanks to his continuous intake of the magic water. The Mayor did see him as a possible asset, *if* his heart and head were in the right place these days.

Dice had already made up his mind. He wasn't waiting a second longer. "I'm going to help. I can't believe we're even sitting here like some peaceful tribe of Indians or rabbits or hares who don't believe in war. We're from Chicago! We gotta go in there and show them just how tough we are. Ain't nobody takin' anything from N.J.R.C. that the Mayor don't want them to take. Besides, we can't leave the boss all on his own either, even if he is some kind of giant. Don't know if his brain ever got any bigger."

Just as Dice finished, Rush ran up to Wrigley. "Wrigley, you've got to help me. My brother, he's headed there now, too, to fight. I don't know what happened. My Uncle Harvey and Mr. Buckingham, Bobbiteer's dad, they were supposed to take them to the beach. But I know they've all gone to fight." She tugged at his right shoulder. "C'mon. They might have guns!"

"Sure, Rush, c'mon, let's go. I won't let anything happen to your brother, I promise." Then he turned to all the rest of the South-Siders. "You heard Dice and the little lady, let's go!" Putz was lagging behind, so Bronzey yelled at him to lose the junk he was carrying around and catch up. He dropped a couple of items he had found earlier and started hopping.

Fuzzy looked at Mugsey and said, "You know the Mayor told us all to stay out of it, since we couldn't zap ourselves invisible yet like his town rabbits can. Maybe we…"

But Mugsey and Meigs both cut him off. "We should have been there already. We're family. We stick together. You know that." Meigs frowned at Fuzzy.

"Yeah, yeah, I know. You're right. I'm comin'. Let's go claim us a victory fight."

In the midst of all the turmoil and potential danger, Rush managed to give Wrigley a smile. She just hoped with all her heart that she could really count on him.

Chapter Nineteen: Charging Forward, Fighting Back

"Bossy, wake up. Wake up, Boss, Chuck says it's time. We're ready to rock and roll!" Wiley shook Bossy gently because he knew he'd get walloped if he wasn't careful.

Kincaid grumbled, smacked his lips, and sat upright behind the steering wheel. He rubbed his eyes. "Well it's about time. Let's go get us some water, boys." He turned the ignition key and his truck was ready to charge forward.

The tanker hummed loudly. Chuck motioned for Bossy to follow him and Jeff, and he set the wheels of altercation in motion. As far as he knew and had discovered from Bossy's (well, Zach's) map, one back road would take them pretty close to the artesian well. Chuck hoped he didn't have to drive on sand. The chance of getting stuck in the desert wasn't his idea of a fun summer evening in Bruneau.

Wiley and Casey were grinning from ear to ear and their hearts were pounding to the beat of a jamming country song. They sat upright, too, in the front seat of the pickup right next to Bossy, but were just tall enough to see out the windows.

"Casey, take a good look at me and a good look in that rearview mirror there. It's the last time we'll be fittin' in this truck without almost touchin' our heads to the ceiling like the boss here." Casey looked in the mirror real quick and smiled.

"Wiley, hand me that there bottle on the floor there, will ya? I just need a sip or two. Tryin' to stay on my best behavior here, keep alert, ya know, so I can help you all fight these giant wild rabbits." Wiley obliged. Bossy took four swigs and gave the bottle back.

Chuck and Jeff were leading the way. "Jeff, you got that rifle of mine all set to go? I should a brung my double barrel shotgun, too, just in case."

"Got it, Chuck. Hey, we won't really have to do any shootin', will we? All they gotta do is hand over the water. You heard the giant tellin' us it ain't no use on cows. Maybe he's tellin' the truth. Bossy's gonna get us in a whole big mess a trouble for nothin'." He looked over to Chuck for an answer.

"What do we care, long as we get paid. We'll do whatever we got to so's we can get old Bossy his precious water. Ain't up to us if it works or not. He'll pay us soon as we get it for him." He gave Jeff his

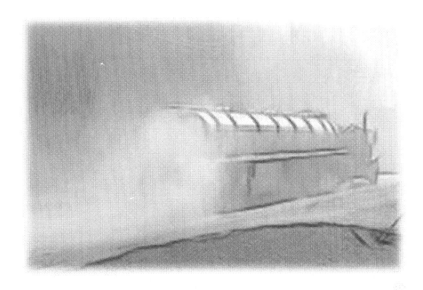

best reassuring look. "Now don't go gettin' soft on us. We gotta charge in there like we mean business!"

"Okay, Chuck, I'm with ya. Hey, look, there's the turnoff coming up, the back road." He pointed to a road heading right. Chuck had to slow the big tanker way down so he could make the turn.

He motioned outside the driver's side window for Bossy to slow down; he was coming up too fast from behind.

It only took another minute and there they sat. Staring out with a peek at the springhouse where they knew the water was located. They were all on the lookout, but they didn't see one giant rabbit. No Mayor, no little rabbits, no six-feet-tall ones neither.

"Somethin' don't feel right, you guys," Bossy Kincaid said. Let's get out and take a look around before we try to go any further." Kincaid, Wiley, and Casey all stepped out and noticed how quiet the desert was and how alone they felt. Chuck and Jeff got out and looked around, too.

Bossy was getting impatient. He knew it would be getting dark in a few hours. "Well there ain't nobody around. Guess that Mayor's gonna just up and let us take the water. He knew we had these here weapons." He waved his rifle up in the air. "Probably don't want none of his precious rabbits gettin' hurt."

Just as he said the word "hurt" though, all five of them heard Mr. Mayor's voice. "I urge you all to leave right this minute, peacefully. If not, I can tie you all up to trees and leave you for the desert animals at night and the hot desert sun in the morning," the Mayor said seriously. Then his voice bounced out into the air from a completely different location. "Bossy, you'll be getting awful thirsty for that bottle by the time the night is over with."

Bossy rubbed his eyes and shook his head not believing what was happening.

"Where's he at, where's he at, Chuck?" Jeff hollered.

"I can't see him, can you?" Chuck answered back as he looked all around.

"Yeah, leave now!" The intruders heard a whole chorus of rabbits shout.

"Where they at? Shoot boys! Just shoot at 'em!" Bossy yelled as he pointed his rifle in the direction of the voices.

"I ain't seein' nothin', Bossy, how the heck am I gonna shoot it?" Chuck yelled back loudly.

Wiley and Casey hopped around looking everywhere for some sign of rabbits, small or giant-sized.

"Fine," Bossy hollered, "you ain't gonna show yourselves, this isn't even a fair fight. We're just goin' in! Load up boys. Let's get a little closer and get the hose out."

"Yeah!" Wiley shouted.

"Yeah!" Casey mimicked. Chuck and Jeff hopped back in the tanker with no problem, but when the others tried to get back into Bossy's pickup, they felt somebody tugging at their kneecaps.

"What the Holy Cow?" Bossy yelled, tumbling to the ground with his partners.

"You aren't going anywhere!" said a different voice. They all heard voices shouting at them. Then they all felt the release from their knees so they could stand up again. Finally the Mayor spoke up. "Now fellas, this is your last chance. We've got you surrounded. You're not going anywhere but out of here."

Jeff jumped up into the tanker and yelled to Chuck, "Let's get the heck outta here, Chuck, please, nobody told us we'd be fightin' invisible ghosts!"

Chuck climbed in as fast as he could, and started the ignition, while Bossy, Wiley, and Casy did the same in the pickup. But Chuck was persistent, unlike Jeff. "Nope, we're goin' in. Bossy, follow me!" he yelled. "CHARGE!"

Mr. Mayor and his invisible Patrol Guards couldn't believe it. The fools were still going to charge in, trample on, and try and soak up a well that wouldn't do them a bit of good.

"Okay, just relax, you've done your part. Just stand by," the ten-rabbit Unit received their orders from their Mayor, their entrusted commander and protector.

As Bossy and the boys thrust their trucks forward a little closer to the springhouse, they looked in the rearview mirror and couldn't believe their eyes. There he was, the big guy, the giant rabbit dressed in those funny clothes again with ten other now visible six-feet-tall hares all wearing T-shirts that read New Jack Rabbit City in big, bold letters.

"What kind of world did we enter into here? Man, this is the real thing, the real live twilight zone!" Jeff shouted.

"I see 'em, I see 'em now," Chuck said, looking in the rearview mirror.

"If we can see 'em, then we can shoot 'em, right pardners!" Bossy slammed his foot on the brake, which he really didn't have to do. He was only traveling at the lowest speed, barely moving. He jumped out of the truck, pointed his rifle and shot directly at the Mayor. He knew he had him. Wiley and Casey jumped out, too.

The bullet left the rifle. Bossy waited for impact with a big satisfying grin on his face. "Yeah, bullseye!"

"He's shootin' at 'em, Chuck, hold up, look, Bossy shot at the big guy!" Chuck stopped the truck and looked back.

A funny pop sound happened, then poof! The Mayor and the other ten rabbits were all invisible again.

"Gosh dang them rabbits, they ain't playin' fair! Just get in the dern truck, let's get us that water!" Bossy ordered.

He threw his rifle in the back of the truck this time. But before they could jump back into the truck, all of a sudden it was raining rocks. Little rocks were being hailed at their windows, at their windshields, and at THEM!

One caught Casey in the left arm. "OW! That hurt." He grabbed his arm and rubbed it, looked down, and saw a rock the size of a walnut, and it had a jagged edge on it, too.

"Fire away kids!" shouted Wyndhameer, as Harvey and the kids stood behind some bushes.

"OW!" Wiley yelled out this time. "There's another one! Got me in the back! Let's get 'em, Boss!"

"Just get in the dern truck you two, let's go get 'em!" Bossy yelled. "Them dirty scoundrels must be slingin' rocks at us! Just keep movin'!"

Over to the left behind the bushes, Wiley thought he saw something. "Look, Boss, behind those bushes there," he pointed. "There's a couple runt rabbit kids standin' there dressed in some kinda silly karate clothes. Where they get off wearin' clothes? And who the heck are those two old geezers by them? Let's get 'em!" Bossy slammed on the brakes again, unnecessarily, and jumped out, forgetting his rifle lying in the back of the truck.

Chuck stopped his truck, too, and looked back to see what was happening.

"I'm tellin' ya, Chuck," Jeff pleaded, "this is crazy, useless, let's just get the heck out of here."

"Ah, sit tight, we ain't the one getting hit by rocks or nothin' and maybe we gotta do some shootin', maybe we don't, but I wanna try and do what we came here for and get that water."

Bossy, Wiley and Casey, all three charged forward right into the line of rock solid fire.

"Fire!" yelled Ryker. He slung a rock off and hit Bossy in the stomach.

"OW! Why you lousy… I oughta…" He grabbed his stomach and took a deep breath, wheezing all the while.

"Fire!" Bobbiteer yelled, hitting Wiley this time, in the left leg, and then Casey's shoulder.

"Good hits kids, but fall back, fall back now!" ordered Wyndhameer. Buckingham and Arlington shielded the kids while they all retreated toward some larger bushes.

Bossy fell over and started grumbling, "Oh my achin' gut. Got me right in the gut. Never mind them scared rabbits. They're runnin' for cover. Help me up. Let's just go get the blasted water." He held out his hands so Wiley and Casey could help him up.

"They got me in the leg!" Wiley whined.

"Well they got me in the shoulder real good. I'm gonna get those guys one a these days. You can bet your magic water on that!" Casey tooted his vengeful yearning.

"C'mon, Bossy! Let's just go get the dern water and get outta here before it gets dark! C'mon!" Chuck yelled loudly with his tanker still idling.

"No deal, I'm gonna skin me some rabbits, if I can see 'em, then I can sure enough run over them with my truck! C'mon, Wiley, Casey, let's go get 'em!" Kincaid and the two accomplices climbed back into the pickup. Kincaid floored it and headed straight for where Bobbiteer, Ryker, Harvey, and Wyn were.

But Kincaid didn't have a chance. Mr. Mayor and his Patrol Guards appeared again and grabbed hold of the back of the pickup and lifted it right off the ground. The back tires just kept spinning while Wyn and Harvey told Bobbit and Ryker to hold off firing to see if Kincaid was ready to give up.

"Yeah," Bobbit yelled, "Have you had enough? Are you gonna take your trucks and get out of here?" He couldn't resist loading up his slingshot again.

"Slingshots, you think you can scare us off with slingshots and pingin' us with a few rocks? And just by makin' my tires spin?" Kincaid laughed. "Wiley, jump back there and get me my rifle. I'll show these kids and old geezers what bullets are really like." It did no good, but Bossy kept flooring the accelerator.

"But, Bossy, them rabbits are back there. I can't..." Wiley said as he and Casey looked scared.

"Well then, right there in my glove box, you get me that there gun a mine. It's ready to go, too. I ain't into shootin' little kid rabbits, but those older ones been askin' for it. Give it here!" he yelled.

Unfortunately, the gun in the glove box was one the Mayor and his rabbits didn't count on. They had managed to fill all the rifles with blanks while invisible, but this one caught them by surprise. Even Mr. Mayor was thinking, "Oh, oh, a real loaded gun here." But he and a few of his invisible guards were already headed for the tanker truck since Chuck was revving the engine up and getting ready to go in.

"Hop back, you kids, hop back! He's got a gun!" Wyndhameer yelled.

But Bobbiteer and Ryker both felt invincible and wanted so badly to play the role of protector. They jumped out in front just as Bossy fired. Wyndhameer and Harvey grabbed at both of them and pulled them back, but the bullet was airborne, on its way. The Mayor zapped himself into position but just seconds too late. Ryker was directly in the line of fire.

That's when Wrigley acted out of pure instinct – he and the other South-Siders got there just in the nick of time, and Wrigley hopped directly in front of all four of them. Bam! The bullet shot into Wrigley's left leg and down he went.

"Wrigley!" Rush screamed, running toward him.

"No, stay back, Rush, he's gonna keep shooting!" Wrigley had one paw up in the air motioning her to stay back and the other one covering the bleeding injury.

Rush didn't listen, still running to Wrigley, but Ryker took a firm hold of her and pulled her back. "No, Sis, no."

"This next one's for you old man!" Bossy fired again, aiming for Harvey.

This time Mr. Mayor was able to snatch the second real bullet right out of mid-air. Then one of his invisible Rabbit Patrol Guards grabbed the gun right from Bossy's hands, but he never saw a thing, just felt it, and the gun was gone.

Wyndhameer, Harvey, the kids, Rush, and all the South-Siders gathered around Wrigley to help him.

With the back of the truck still being held up by some of the Mayor's Unit, Bossy, Wiley and Casey jumped out. Bossy Kincaid kept giving orders, "You two go in and get that water, NOW!"

Mr. Mayor turned to Caponey, the eight-feet-tall, nine-hundred-pound monster-sized rabbit that he'd become.

"Well, Mister Caponey, looks like you're on. They won't listen. We've given them every chance to turn back. Do your thing. I'm – we're – all counting on you," the Mayor said earnestly. "I mean, we could tie them all up and do all sorts of things, but scaring them to the point of no return, that's what we're aiming for. You got it?"

"Got it, Big Guy. Okay ebberybody, this is it. Stand by!" Caponey took charge, while Mr. Mayor and the other rabbits all fell back and decided to let him handle the situation.

Suddenly the N.J.R.C. intruders felt the earth and desert sand shake.

"Holy Cow! Are we havin' an earthquake? Not now, God, we gotta get us that water!" Wiley yelled and whined at the same time.

The attackers all looked back and saw Mr. Mayor standing there again, in plain sight, with his other ten guards. But they were standing very still.

When Chuck turned his head back around and looked forward again, he began to hyperventilate and shake all over. Jeff almost went into immediate shock. Standing right there in front of the truck, staring down on them, was the haunting, threatening sight, the monster-sized Caponey.

Jeff stuttered to get the words out: "There's a double-sized giant angry lookin' bear in the middle of the desert Chuck! What do we do?" His teeth chattered and he swallowed hard so he could breathe.

"That ain't… no bear buddy… look at those ears! That there is one big son-of-a-gun monster RABBIT!" His breathing was so labored he had to count his breaths just so he could still function. "And he's actin' like he's mad or hungry or somethin'!"

Caponey let out a terrifying growl, just like a bear would, a super-sized bear. He lifted his huge arms into the air; then swung them back down as if he was going to slam his fists down on top of the front of the tanker.

"Where... ugh Jeff, oh Jeffy, where... hand me that rifle a mine?" Chuck stammered.

"Oh no, Chuckie, I didn't sign up for this. Bossy can keep his money, I'm outta here! Sorry." He gripped the door handle, counted to three, jumped out of the truck and ran for his life. He whizzed right past Bossy, Wiley, and Casey, and kept on running.

"Why that backpeddlin' no good cowboy! I can't see in front of us 'cause of the tanker. C'mon, boys, let's go! Let's get up there and see what all the fuss is now."

Chuck got brave again, put his foot on the gas peddle and tried to floor the tanker. "Get outta my way you crazy big bundle of fur! I'm comin' through!"

But Caponey had already gotten a good grip on the tanker and lifted the front end right off the ground. The front wheels spun like crazy.

For the first time, Wiley, Casey and Bossy saw the big monster standing there right before their unbelieving eyes. Caponey spent a few seconds picking up the front of the tanker and shaking it right and left. He let it hit hard again as he released his grip.

"Holy *Jack and the Beanstalk*! Will ya look at the size of this big fat monster!" Bossy cried out.

"Fat!" Caponey roared. "Fat!" "This here is all extra muscle and I'm gonna show you what extra muscle can do to a scrawny, mean guy like you!" Caponey stomped his giant legs and feet in the direction of Bossy, but first he yanked the keys from the ignition of the tanker. Chuck didn't make a move. Wiley and Casey felt compelled to try and help somehow although they were scared to death. They both tugged at Caponey's feet, but he just flung them right into the air.

Now feeling defenseless without his gun, it was starting to sink in for old Bossy Kincaid. That old giant rabbit had him a pretty good surprise weapon. But even in the midst of all the failed attacks, thoughts of his cows growing huge like Caponey and bringing in the profits floated into his delusional brain. Wiley's, too. Casey, not so much. He didn't care anymore. He just wanted to live!

Chuck gave up now, too. He hopped out, ran for his life and didn't look back. Hated to think what was gonna become of old Bossy Kincaid and his two poor talking, scheming rabbit friends.

But Bossy just didn't want to give up. The Mayor and his Patrol Guard Unit just stayed back out of the way and let Caponey handle the battle at this point. Bossy Kincaid mouthed off again and started punching Caponey in the legs.

Wiley and Casey, still dizzy, just sat down, gave up, and watched.

"You little drunken, punchin' fool." Caponey picked Bossy up like he was a toothpick, then slapped him back down on the ground. "Now are you gonna hightail it outta here and leave this nice society they got goin' on here alone, or not?"

"Or not!" Bossy sassed back. "I'm gonna get me some more help and more guns and rifles, come back, and make you bleed, you over-sized fat furry soldier wannabe!" He made a run for his truck.

Caponey shook his head in disbelief and shrugged his giant shoulders. "This guy ain't givin' up, Mr. Mayor. Hey all you South-Siders, get over here, let's show him what he's facin' if he don't leave this place in peace!"

Rush stayed with Wrigley and wrapped Ryker's karate T-shirt around his wound. She couldn't believe her brother gave it to her to use. Mr. Buckingham and Mr. Arlington told Ryker and Bobbiteer to stay put, that they'd helped enough, while the other South-Siders started hopping toward Caponey to join in scaring Bossy Kincaid out of the dunes. Mr. Mayor spoke up, though, and said, "You let your boss handle this. He's doing just fine. I've got my reasons." And they did, even though the South-Siders were not used to taking orders from anybody but Caponey, and after all, he'd told them to stay put back at the campsite, since none of them had decided to drink the water and grow big. Caponey'd figured he and Mr. Mayor, and his rabbits with their powers to disappear, would do the trick.

But Dice wasn't listening to anybody except his buddy, Caponey. He hopped right up to him and said, "I'm here, Boss. Right here with ya. Let's get 'em."

Wiley and Casey watched as Bossy made a run for his truck. When Caponey turned and looked at them to see if they had come to their senses, the two scared rabbits put their paws high into the air in surrender.

Then, just in an instant, for true war-battle momentum changes in a heartbeat, all of a sudden, for once, it was Caponey who was in jeopardy. Chuck, a former marine, knew he had to go back. He couldn't leave a man behind, even if it was a man like Bossy. He had made a U-turn, hopped up into the back of Bossy's pickup, loaded Kincaid's bow and arrow, and aimed it straight for Caponey's head. A monster rabbit that size, he figured, was a danger to society, and he had an obligation to at least wound Caponey. He fired the arrow off. The guards looked at Mr. Mayor, but he shook his head no, so nobody intervened.

Then Caponey heard a shout from Dice. "Boss, duck! DUCK, BOSS!" So instinctively Caponey bent his big head and tall ears forward. Again, the Mayor told his guards to stand down, he'd take care of it, so he snatched the arrow right out of mid-air and immediately crushed it into dust. Caponey knew it could have meant an eyeball being darted out.

The angry South-Siders all rushed to battle it out with Chuck, and had him tied up in no time with some rope. The Mayor kept telling his Unit to "stand down" because he knew this was a great chance for Caponey to live through some, perhaps, life-changing moments, feel good about himself, and finally start changing his ways. The same for the rest of the South-Siders.

Dice and the others yelled out to Caponey, "Don't worry, Boss, we got this guy, you get Kincaid." Chuck heard Dice, looked down and there he was, the little scrawny black and white rabbit and the other ones, too, all staring at him. Chuck lifted up his tied legs and tried to stomp his boots down on Dice. So Dice chomped down and bit his right leg straight through his blue jeans, just below the knee. "That's what you get for tryin' to mess with my boss!" Meigs and Bronzey actually gave Dice a hug. Fuzzy, Mugsey, and Putz just shook their heads, couldn't believe all that was happening.

Finally the Mayor gave an order for his guards to contribute, join in the battle again. As far as the Mayor's Unit, they couldn't understand why there was even a battle going on. After all, Mr. Mayor had his magical ways, but they all figured he had a reason for letting it all play out the way it did. He usually did have his reasons, philosophical perspectives and explanations for everything that happened.

"Hurry up, get that guy Chuck out of here!" the Mayor commanded. "Some war vet, what a disgrace. And get those other two little rascal rabbits, too! Take them and drop them right back off in town and tell them what will happen if they ever come back: it's mouse-size for them with the use of our one well. Make sure you show them an example of just how we can do that, too, got it?"

The Mayor's rabbit Unit went to work.

"Oh yeah, and make sure you tell them all we want is peace and love here, that's it. And we offer that to them, too. But if they come around again *disturbing* the peace, they'll get nothing but *tough* love. Okay, take 'em away."

But Bossy was still free, and with two more steps he thought he'd have it made. He'd hop in his truck, go into town and bring a whole army of people who wouldn't mind being paid good money to battle it out with a crazy town of tall, talking rabbits.

He yelled out to Caponey, "You'll see, I'll get me some hired guns, and if that don't work, we'll bring along some dynamite and blow this whole blasted desert up! If I can't have the water, nobody will!"

But it wasn't to be. Like an electric shock, all of a sudden Kincaid felt terrible jabbing pains in his chest. He could barely catch his breath. He fell over and grabbed at his heart. He knew it was all over.

"My ticker," he gasped. "Not again." The old man screamed out in pain as he stretched his other hand toward the door handle of his truck. "Help, Chuck! Wiley! Help me! It's my dern heart again... I can't..." But they couldn't help anybody, they were being hauled off with the other culprit, Casey, back to town, according to Mr. Mayor's orders.

Caponey came to a stop and stared down at the weak, hurting fellow lying in the sand right next to the pickup. Mr. Mayor came over, all the other rabbits, even Bobbit and Ryker from where they were hiding. Mr. Mayor gave them a scornful look. He knew they were not supposed to be there. Then he saw Wyndhameer and Harvey and gave them a quick nod.

"Well, Caponey, what do you think, should we call in an ambulance for this guy or not?" the Mayor said in jest, knowing very well they would help the poor soul.

"I know CPR, can I help?" Bobbiteer quickly kneeled down by Kincaid and got in position to save a life, a life you had to wonder if it was worth it.

"Do your thing, kid," the Mayor motioned to him.

Bobbit started in with compressions. He wasn't putting his mouth on the old man's mouth, no way. He had taken a first aid/CPR rabbit class once and learned that compressions would do just fine to keep things going until the haremedics arrived. He locked his paws in place as he was taught and started compressing.

"Well, guess if you're gonna save this guy's life, I'll make the 9-1-1 call, get the human medics out here for him and the haremedics real quick for Wrigley there. I can give them our location. I saw a phone inside his truck."

But first the Mayor did something nobody expected. He kneeled down beside Bossy Kincaid and whispered to him. "Love, my friend, not greed, that's what saves a day. Think of your gal, Maxie. She'll be waiting for you when you change your ways. Keep breathing."

Bobbiteer kept the compressions going and Bossy kept on breathing.

Meanwhile, Caponey got a chance to thank his buddy, Dice. "Dice, hey, buddy, I told you to stay outta this. The Mayor and his guys and I was supposed to take care of it. There was too much danger with the guns and all. What you wanna come and get yourself caught up in this for?"

"Ah, I just thought ya might need an extra hand or a bite or somethin'. Besides, I owed ya, Boss. A life for a life, remember? You uncaged me, set me free. I could never forget that!"

The rest of the South-Siders gathered around Caponey, Dice and the others.

"All of you, thanks for your help. Hey, I think that frequency is makin' me talk smarter. I said *you*, not *yous*, what do ya know!" Caponey laughed, and the earth shook.

And that was that, the end of the Desert Stormer's crusade to capture the magic water. With Bossy down, incapacitated by his heart attack, and being threatened by Caponey and the Mayor, Chuck and Jeff gave up the notion of stealing magic water. There was no way they were facing Caponey again.

Wiley and Casey? Well, needless to say, they did NOT want to be reduced to mouse-size. Better to be a regular-sized rabbit than not one at all, or tiny like a mouse. So they moved on with their lives.

When Caponey and Wrigley got back to N.J.R.C. and their campsites, they were treated like heroes, but they told it like it was, how Dice, Mr. Mayor, his Unit, and all the others really came through, too. The worrying stopped for Brooklyn, Annie and Miranda, now that all the kids and husbands were back in one piece. It took hours of asking for forgiveness from Wyndhameer and Harvey, though, since they had done something so "idiotic and irresponsible," as Miranda put it, putting the kids in danger the way they did.

But Bobbiteer and Ryker actually got the last say, without having to utter a word. The bond between parent and sons was never stronger and both Miranda and Brooklyn would be forever grateful for that. Bobbiteer wasn't begging to go home anymore, either. He said he had the best day ever.

One little tug and Mr. Mayor had that bullet out of Wrigley's leg so he could start healing up, with Rush right by his side. All of the other South-Siders were glad everything turned out all right and headed for their campsite.

Caponey grinned and patted Dice on the shoulder as they walked away. "Mr. Mayor knew what he was doing. I think he might a even figured in about old Kincaid havin' a heart condition. He knew he wouldn't last a fight with the likes of me. He's a smart guy, that big fella."

"Hey, Cap, remember what you said before? You didn't think you liked bein' all this tall? You gonna go back to normal size or what?" Dice looked up at him.

"Ah, the Mayor already told me he'd help me out with another magic water potion. I'm thinkin' six feet is plenty tall enough, what do you think, Dice?"

"Yeah, plenty big, I'd say. I still ain't decided if I wanna get tall or not."

"Oh you're standin' tall already, Dice, you're standin' tall already."

"Ah jeez, thanks, Boss." Dice started blushing and hung his humble head down.

"Hey, the big guy says he's takin' down the sign, and all of us are gonna have to drink enough of that one water potion, stay invisible for the most part around here, so we don't have no more troubles, for a while anyway. I figure we'll stay invisible, except for emergencies, if we gotta scare the wits outta any more a them desert invaders. And my Rappers, of course they gotta show themselves. Now how are they doin'? They still workin' on that one song, '*Love Conquers All*'?" Caponey laughed and shook the earth again. "Man, I'm tired, I gotta lie down, get me some shut-eye and dream a little."

Dice nestled up beside Caponey and stared at him. He couldn't believe he was so big. "Okay, Boss. Get some rest. But hey, just one more thing. If Bronzey, Meigs, Fuzzy and Mugsey do get big and famous, did the Mayor say how he'd keep this place from becomin' one chaotic tourist attraction? I mean wouldn't all of us have to show ourselves so people could see us and know this was our home now?"

"Ah, Dice, you worry too much. Mr. Mayor's a smart fella. He'll figure it all out." He paused, then added, "Thanks again, Corporal Dice, for being there today."

Dice laughed. "Sure thing, Colonel Caponey, or are we still callin' ya, King Caponey?"

"Just Caponey's fine. After all, I'm just one a you South-Sider's, right?"

Caponey yawned several times, shut his eyes, fell asleep, and dreamed of counting all the money he'd be making as manager for his talented rock stars, The Rappin' Rabbits.

It wasn't long before stars and a crescent moon lit up the clear blue Idaho sky. Later that night, when Caponey, the South-Siders, the Chicago Hares and all the other rabbits and Mayor of N.J.R.C. were sleeping good because they didn't have to worry anymore—Rush and Wrigley sat on the beach, held each other tight, and hugged and kissed. With earphones on, they took turns listening to the love songs they had recorded for each other. The last song of the night, though, was a tune they just knew would be a hit soon. They closed their eyes and sang the words.

Chicago hares moved west ya see.
Jack Rabbit City's the place to be.
Left the South side, wild side,
the Loop and Lake Shore Drive,
that one and only skyline.
But Idaho's workin' out for us.
It's all turnin' out just fine.

"I love you, Rush Palmer," Wrigley said.

"I love you, too." Rush replied. "It's beautiful here in the desert, isn't it?"

"Yes it is, my love, yes it is. Just like you."

LOVE SPARKS (Wrigley, I love you)

Wrigley, I love you. Wrigley, I do.
I truly, truly love you. Yes, I really do.
Wrigley, I love you. Wrigley, I do.
I truly, truly love you. Yes, I really do.

Yes I do, yes I do.
I truly, truly love you.
Yes I really do.
Yes I do, yes I do.
I truly, truly love you.
Yes I really do, yes I do.
Yes I do. Wrigley, I love you.
Yes I truly do. Yes I do.

You make me happy.
You make me smile.
I used to feel so lost and sad,
but not for quite a while.

'Cause Wrigley I love you,
Wrigley I do.
I truly, truly love you,
yes I really do.
Yes I do, yes I do.
Wrigley, I love you.
Yes I truly do.
Yes I do, yes I do.
Wrigley, I love you.
Yes I truly do, yes I do.

Now you say you love me.
I know you really do.
Stay with me forever.
Please say you'll make it true.

Wrigley, I love you.
Wrigley, I do.
Stay with me forever.
Please say you'll make it true.
Make it true. Make it true.
Stay with me forever.
Please say you'll make it true.
Make it true, make it true.

Stay with me forever,
Please say you'll make it true.
Make it true, make it true.
Stay with me forever.
Please say you'll make it true.

LOVE CONQUERS ALL

When we're faced with adversity
here in New Jack Rabbit City,
we gear up with love.
'Cause love conquers all.
That way we know for sure,
we're truly standing tall.

So gear up, stand up, get ready to fight.
But only if you have to, defend your rights.
Battles are no fun, no fun at all.
Gear up with love, 'cause love conquers all.

Fight only with the best intentions.
That way, you're fightin'
within patriotic dimensions.
For instance, we didn't kill, we just disarmed.
We didn't kill, we just disarmed.
Stood our ground, with nobody harmed.
Stood our ground, with nobody harmed.

So gear up, stand up, get ready to fight.
But only if you have to, defend your rights.
Battles are no fun, no fun at all.
Gear up with love, 'cause love conquers all.

Even compassion for old Bossy,
his fate and bad heart.
Told him it was useless, right from the start.
He'll have to learn the hard way now,
how to get smart.
He'll have to learn the hard way now,
how to sober up and get smart.

Special thanks to Caponey
and Mister Mayor, our kings.
Thanks Caponey for coming around.
Thanks Mr. Mayor, for everything.

Feels good to be good, doesn't it Boss?
For once the boss was at a loss.
Didn't know how he felt inside.
He just knew it had somethin' to do with pride.
He knew it had somethin' to do with pride.

Just a reminder.
We're The Rappin' Rabbits, ya see.
Got us a new home and life,
all 'cause we moved out here
to New Jack Rabbit City.

Gonna protect it too, with love,
then just let it be, just let it be.
'Cause love conquers all,
here in New Jack Rabbit City.

Love conquers all, love.
Love conquers all, love.
Love conquers all, love.
Love conquers all, love.

Chapter 20: What the World Needs Now

"Yes sir, that's what I always say and live by, and I love the way Dusty Springfield sang it, 'What the world needs now is love, sweet love. It's the only thing that there's just too little of,'" Mr. Mayor professed as he stood by the hemlock tree, early the next morning, to give his victory speech the day after Kincaid and his partners (in wishful crime) disturbed the peace. He gave a short pep talk; then thanked his Unit, Caponey, Wrigley, and everyone else for "standing tall" in a day of crisis. As he wrapped up his wisdom in a nutshell, he spoke a few last words. "Yes sir, keep love and hope in your hearts folks; that's what life is all about."

The mood amongst all of the residents of N.J.R.C. could only be summed up with two words—serenity and exuberance. Pure joy glowed on every rabbit and hare in the dunes that day. Many still talked about the exciting events from the battle they had just all fought together and the fact that N.J.R.C. inhabited a noble hare like Wrigley who would take a bullet for the one he loved. Not only that, but everyone enjoyed the company of a monster-sized celebrity-status hero, too, the unlikely revised of heart and soul one and only, Caponey.

Oh, he joked to Dice, all the other South-Siders, and even the Mayor, when he was asked to say a few words, how he wasn't no hero, "just a reformed citizen on board now, in the Good Ship Lollipop land where Mr. Mayor guides ebberybody toward the pathways of goodness." Caponey even admitted that, at first, all he could think about was fighting against Bossy so he could keep all the precious water for himself. Then he added, "I won't be surprised if we all find a yellow brick road bein' built next, here in N.J.R.C., since Mr. Mayor has all of us changin' our ways and keeps fine-tunin' the goodness in us all. Pretty soon, the only adversity we'll all be facin' is some windstorms. I can't see crime bein' a problem here in our new city we now all claim as home." Everyone cheered as he finished his short speech.

All the South-Siders and Chicago hares, they just couldn't believe how different their lives were now. Ryker and Bobbiteer weren't happy with the "can't grow tall until later" rule, but they figured they could wait it out. Mrs. Palmer felt like a rabbit out of her familiar city habitat, but loved the effect the desert and the Mayor was having on her kids. Rush had found true love and Wrigley finally got his acceptance and the girl of his dreams. The Arlingtons and Buckinghams were so thrilled with the peaceful life they had chosen, chased, and found. They frolicked about with so much more bounce in their hop and hope in their hearts now.

Putz, the junk collecting South-Sider, still stuck to himself a lot, kind of got lost in the shuffle of the new desert life, but it was okay with him. He thought he had died and gone to heaven. Nothing like a beach with lost treasures in the sand to let him enjoy his hobby and reap the rewards of one rule he finally saw the merit in—finders' keepers.

The Rappin' Rabbits' foursome: Bronzey, Meigs, Fuzzy and Mugsey felt honored to sing at the end of the celebration speech. All four quoted some of their poetic lyrics and conveyed this message: "There are a "million songs in a life yet to be sung, a million miles in a life yet to be run." They, too, praised: Caponey, Wrigley, Mr. Mayor, his dedicated Unit, and the "Karate Kids" (that's what they nicknamed Bobbiteer and Ryker). They thanked all the rabbits for welcoming them and keeping New Jack Rabbit City a magical, peaceful place.

Of course, the human family wanted to celebrate the happy ending, too. They'd heard in town what had happened, and showed up at N.J.R.C. early the next morning to congratulate the Mayor. So after The Rappin' Rabbits sang, Abby got the surprise of her life.

Mr. Mayor asked *her* to say a few words about how to keep believing in yourself and the powers of imagination, and why nobody should ever give up. With a lump in her little throat, she went right ahead and did just that! Inspired everyone. Nothing like an eight-year-old sweet girl like Abby to help rabbits and humans tune into the ideals of potential and ultimate realms of possibility.

Yet she was the one who felt inspired. After all, she said, "My brother, uncle, and I are standing here before you on the grains of sand of this magical kingdom where anything is possible. All I can say, all *we* can say, is thanks for the inspiration, for the wonderful magic. I'll always believe in magic. I'll always believe, just because of all of you." She threw the Mayor and crowd a kiss and ran back to stand beside Zach, her Uncle Mike, and the two dogs. Eggy and Nasty's tails wagged like crazy. Mike hugged her and Zach gave her a high five.

The sun beat down, but the desert's soft breeze and wondrous feeling in everyone's hearts made for a perfect day. As the crowd dispersed, Caponey walked alongside Dice.

"Hey, Dice, what do ya think of me as the Mayor when old giant ears steps down and retires? I could run this town like Daley did in the old days. I bet the bennys and perks the big guy gets gotta be awesome. Yeah, I can see it now: Mayor Caponey at your service, running the city the way it should be. Of course, only thing we'll be fightin' against is maybe some windstorms, like I said before, not much crime, since the Mayor has everybody hoppin' 'On the Good Ship Lollipop' trail. Hey, I did it again, I said *everybody*! That's how ya say it, right? So what do ya think, buddy?" He patted Dice on his head; then in one quick move hoisted him up onto his shoulders.

Dice smiled, held on, and with an air of equality finally answered. "Guess we could talk to Mr. Mayor about that someday, but, Boss, we're livin' the good life for now and I know you're changin' some of your ways, but I've been meanin' to tell ya—you don't know jack."

Caponey laughed and the two of them, along with everyone else within the city limits of N.J.R.C., wandered off to enjoy beautiful Bruneau sunny days, sunsets, and new beginnings.

Caponey had to get the last word in, though. "I'm changin' my ways, changin' my ways. But you're right, buddy, my little honest advisor and friend—I don't know jack!"

The End

DREAMS GOT A WAY OF FINDIN' YOU
(Meigs and Bronzey with Fuzzy and Mugsey)

When I was just a little hare, my momma said to me:
"Bronzy, Meigs, when you grow up, what do you want to be?"
We dreamed, we dreamed, we dreamed, we did.
Our wishes never came true. Not back then, not 'till now.
But dreams got a way of findin' you.

Dreams got a way of findin' you.
Yes they do, yes they do, yes they do.
Dreams got a way of findin' you.
Yes they do, yes they do, yes they do.

Dreams got a way, dreams got a way,
dreams got a way of findin' you.
Dreams got a way, dreams got a way,
dreams got a way of findin' you.

When we were just little ones, our papas said to us:
"Life's rough. Get tough, Son, for all that's about to come."
And so on and so on, we both grew up.
We got older and wiser and sad. Not cool, just sad.
Took wrong turns, took wrong turns and shamed our dads.

But we're all here to tell you,
to go ahead and reach for the stars.
No matter, no matter who you are,
heal that big hole in your heart.

'Cause dreams got a way of findin' you.
Yes they do, yes they do, yes they do.
Dreams got a way of findin' you.
Yes they do, yes they do, yes they do.
Maybe not now, not then.
But quit askin' why, your soul wants to fly.
So give your dreams a try.

'Cause dreams got a way, dreams got a way,
dreams got a way of findin' you.
Dreams got a way, dreams got a way,
dreams got a way of findin' you.
Dreams got a way!

Epilogue

Abby, Zach, Lori, I, and our two dogs visited N.J.R.C. many times within the last year. As far as I know, these occasions are the only times Mr. Mayor and the other residents show themselves. Well, besides when the singers perform in one city or another, or appear as guests on television shows. The kids all have autographed shirts from The Rappin' Rabbits: Bronzey, Meigs, Fuzzy, and Mugsey. Zach and Abby have become quite good friends with Bobbiteer, Ryker, Rush, and Wrigley. If we happen to run into Caponey and Dice, Zach always wants to sit down with them and hear the story again, how they, along with Wrigley and everyone else, saved the day.

Recently, this past Easter, we received a letter in the mail, no stamp, no return address. Just this, from Mr. Mayor:

To My Favorite Human Family:

Greetings from New Jack Rabbit City. I hope this finds you all well. Please enjoy these enclosed tickets for an upcoming summer concert. What are those dogs of yours up to? Abby, Zach, how is school? Please tell Abby that her friend, Rush, has completed the lyrics to the song they worked on together, and The Rappin' Rabbits are almost finished with the tune. Here is the final draft. I can't wait for the talented foursome to sing it someday. Mike and Lori, the next Hare vs. Dog competition is coming up in early autumn. Check with me the next time you folks come to visit.

Fondly,

Mr. Mayor

Abby was thrilled to read the lyrics to us all; she'd been keeping it a big secret. But that's not what got her jumping up and down with excitement—all four of us were suddenly the proud owners of front row seat tickets to a summer concert at the Arie Crown Theatre at

McCormick's Place in Chicago. The Rappin' Rabbits will be opening for the band, One Direction.

Upon arrival of the tickets, Abby went to her room and daydreamed for two days. Zach just rolled his eyes at her every time she gloated about being a songwriter or whenever she mentioned Harry Styles. But I'm getting off the track. Let me tell you what's happening with the rest of the people and rabbits or hares, as I've learned first hand from the Mayor or others in N.J.R.C., or from Abby, and whatever I've heard around town or read in the paper:

Bossy is in a nursing home recovering from the heart attack he incurred trying to fight with the monster-sized rabbit, Caponey. The nursing staff checks anyone who visits him, so nobody can sneak him in any liquor. He's sobered up because of that. Maxie visits often for somebody who says she doesn't care a thing about Bossy Kincaid. Somehow, she's talked him into selling all his cows and switching to the profitable business of processing Ore-Ida potatoes.

Chuck and Jeff are content to run Bossy's business, and they must pay themselves well to be driving brand new trucks around town. It isn't as if their boss can put up much of a fuss, since he's still convalescing. I heard they never wanted to see that monster rabbit, Caponey, again. One night at a restaurant, though, I overheard them talking and they told two of their buddies that they did return, just once, and when they walked through the dunes, they didn't even see a wild bunny rabbit. All they saw were the leaves on the old hemlock tree rustling in the wind.

Wiley and Casey finally got their chance to grow big, thanks to the Mayor's forgiving heart and generous offer to the magic water. I heard they hopped on a freight train bound for California. Wiley has a couple of friends out there who promised him he'd get rich. His buddies found a few gold nuggets and just know there's a bunch more; all they had to do was recruit some more gold panhandlers. Wiley and Casey were happy to oblige. Besides, Wiley probably wants to scare the beJesus out of his pals by showing up as a five-feet-tall rabbit. (That's the height he aspired to, figuring it was plenty big enough, and the Mayor was happy to oblige since Wiley promised to high hare-tail it out of town.)

Caponey and Dice, as acting managers of The Rappin' Rabbits are, in fact, getting rich. Caponey did ask for one more favor from the Mayor. Eight feet tall was just too darn uncomfortable, so he asked if he could get downsized to six feet. After drinking a doctored potion for a few days, sure enough, Caponey got his wish.

Putz turned kind of spiritual and wrote a song thanking God, says he feels as if he is truly "livin' the good life now." His famous singing South-Sider friends set a tune to it and let Putz record it. Once in a while, we'll see him at the beach with a metal detector collecting some interesting treasures in the sand. One time we saw him dancing. He always looks so happy.

Wrigley, according to Abby, confessed to Rush that it wasn't merely a crush he had on her, but "the real thing, a wonderful, lasting love." Abby figures it was the harsh reality of losing their parents at a young age that made Rush and Wrigley decide to start a grief support group, and a tough-love obstacle course where other hares can learn to trust, love again, and heal.

Rush is obviously in love with Wrigley, too. She continues to write in her journal. She hopes to complete a novel someday about New Jack Rabbit City, Mr. Mayor, the residents, all the South-Siders, our family, and even the dogs. One day she told Abby, "Besides writing, I'm also going to become a hare cardiologist someday. You should always aspire to be whatever you want to be, too, and work hard at it."

Brooklyn Palmer seemed happy for all the positive transformations in her son, daughter, and Wrigley. The family appeared closer than ever when I saw them last. I think it's probably after seeing Rush so happy that Mrs. Palmer may have started believing in love again herself. There is talk that she finds one particular rabbit in town interesting and very handsome. She loves her job as a family counselor, and everyone turns to her for advice. All of the other hares and rabbits see how happy her family is now and the way Ryker and Rush make her so proud. They are growing up to be quite good hare role models.

Annie Arlington and ***Miranda Buckingham*** teach a class on cooking a nutritious hare/rabbit diet. They're also working on a cookbook.

Harvey Arlington and Wyndhameer Buckingham are enjoying their jobs as construction workers, and refereeing for the obstacle course races. They take walks on the beach with their wives, and go fishing with Ryker and Bobbiteer. Their latest construction project was a Karate Fitness Studio for the kids, which is now completed. But it's the funniest thing, look inside the windows of the new studio and you can't see anything at all, yet we can hear voices yelling out. Only invisible rabbits and hares practice there. Mr. Mayor explained that it's to keep them physically fit, busy with something positive, and without getting hurt. He said, "Exercise is a natural magic for kids and it is essential for others, too. For many of those who chose to grow big and stand upright, slowly walking around from here to there does not keep them fit. They've gotten lazy."

Ryker and Bobbiteer love to show other young rabbits and hares tricks of the trade, super kicks and fancy moves with their arms and bodies, which will help work the lazy ones back into shape. They told Zach that their magical powers to remain invisible rabbits and zap into being visible are the best weapons in the world, but Mr. Mayor and Wyndhameer keep reminding them that "love is actually the best weapon." Ryker and Bobbiteer also keep up with their school studies. Their parents, Mayor, and good teachers make certain of that.

The Rappin' Rabbits singing foursome, with help from their managers, Caponey and Dice, have become more popular than Alvin and the Chipmunks. Already they have three hit songs, and have just started work on their first album. As the story goes, David Letterman's son, Harry, told his dad one day that somebody, named Caponey, had called and wanted to talk to him about The Rappin' Rabbits appearing on *The Late Show* before he retired. Harry loved the rabbits and their music, so sure enough, they got booked. What a dream come true for the gangster South-Siders who came such a long way from their hardscrabble lives in the alleyways of Chicago, Illinois.

Mr. Mayor often leans up against the old hemlock tree in N.J.R.C. He looks as if he is reflecting, feeling proud as he watches his town grow into one of the finest cities in Idaho. Most of the wayward rabbits and hares have either left town or changed for the better. He took down the N.J.R.C. sign. The Mayor and his advisors all thought it best if residents remained invisible, for the most part. Still, many people believe in the magical kingdom, even if they can't see it. They also made an ordinance mandating young hares and rabbits to remain on a regular water formula that maintains their normal growth rate until they are young adults, when it will be their choice whether to drink from the magic water spring that will enable them to become taller.

The Mayor continues to hold the obstacle course race events. Everybody loves the excitement of the fascinating chases. Once in a while Eggy and Nasty join in the fun, but it's as if Mr. Mayor put a spell on them. They don't seem as competitive anymore, but just run to have fun.

Back in Chicago, Caponey heard from one of his more reliable sources that the North-Sider hare gang is as happy as can be now that the South-Siders are gone and not coming back. Dice said, "It's fine with me and the boss if the North-Siders have all the dirty business and alleyways of Chicago to themselves now. What we'll remember is the way the moonlight glistens over Lake Michigan and the Chicago skyline at night."

One last note: I do see many tall rabbits when we visit, but the only one from Chicago who chose to drink the magic water was Caponey. He told Bronzey, Meigs, Fuzzy and Mugsey that they wouldn't be near as cute if they got big, and they agreed. Zach said Ryker and Bobbiteer are thinking about it, though, when they get older.

Finally, here are the lyrics to Rush and Abby's song.

A MILLION SONGS

There's a secret about life
that I long to tell you
and I hope with all my heart,
it serves to compel you, to dream,
yes to dream.

A million songs in a heart yet to be sung.
A million miles in a life yet to be run.
So spend the day with the sun,
the night with the moon,
your dreams waiting to come true.
If you never wish, if you never dream,
you'll never truly let yourself be you.

A million miles from the past,
a million memories to last.
Though yesterdays are gone, there's still todays
and hopeful hearts find heartfelt ways.

But time waits for no one.
Life keeps moving along.
Todays and tomorrows are for someone.
Yesterdays are cherished, but they're gone.

So spend the day with the sun,
the night with the moon,
your dreams waiting to come true.
If you never wish, if you never dream,
you'll never truly let yourself be you.

Though dreams can be shattered,
it's trying again that matters.
Build castles in the air
and follow through with care.

The sun will keep you warm,
the moon will still your soul.
The stars will be reminders of your dreams.
The stars will be reminders of your dreams.

Made in the USA
Columbia, SC
03 September 2018